The Wilderness Camp Murders

By W.L.W. Borowiecki

The content, incidents, and persons described in this book are entirely fictional in intent and description. Any names of, or similarities to people or persons, living or dead, or current or past entities, is completely unintended and or purely coincidental. Some of the locations and entities mentioned in this story are real, but are only used as a setting for the fictional events of this book, nothing more, and should not be seen as, or meant to be, deleterious or denigrating comments about those locales or entities.

The chapters in this book were previously published as a serial, i.e., chapter-by-chapter, on Amazon Kindle Vella under the same title "The Wilderness Camp Murders".

ISBN 9798390646564

The earth had remade itself into a new world; The Great Upheaval saw to that. Continents had changed shapes while oceans had spread. On a smaller scale, the violence that often grows out of human egos and competition was gone, and the world was finally at peace.

"Suddenly there was a shriek from the little bath house and we all looked over there. Sukey was in the doorway and she called out shakily "I found the knife"."

Murder had visited The Wilderness Camp.

Follow EG's and Mrs. Lambskin's journal as they accidentally uncover the secrets of their new social order created after The Great Upheaval while attempting to identify the killer of three of their friends.

Table of Contents

Chapter 1 – *The First Day, or, How It All Started*

I'm just not sure what really happened that last week in August. Since I've always enjoyed writing down my thoughts and experiences, that's what this is, my version of what happened out there and hopefully they'll let me use this at my murder trial later this week.

It was warm out there in the woods and we were there for the "Woodsman Graduation" training class; basically, I, along with the others from my high school graduating class, were plunked out in the middle of nowhere in the northern territory to learn 'how to survive in the wild' or rather, basic life-skills. In addition, we'd be tested on the other things we've been taught in school like knitting and sewing (which comes in handy for working in the town clothing factory), cooking, house construction and wood-working techniques, and basic and emergency medical care. Yeah, it was kinda like one of those survival classes they say one used to pay a whole lot of dollars to attend, but we were there to gain the necessary skills to live in today's modern world, and as it was part of our adulthood training, it didn't cost anything. Besides, today's modern world isn't all that modern anymore compared to what I've heard some of the old people talk about.

Briefly, from what we were taught in school, ever since the great fault off the western coast ruptured, which set off a series of earthquakes and other fault zone ruptures, what used to be the west coast of the old Amerca pretty much dissolved. New mountains appeared off the coast, big inland areas sank and became large bays of the great western ocean, and huge amounts of people died, either in the first onslaught of earthquakes or in the ensuing mayhem in the following weeks and months. Then hundreds of millions, perhaps even billions, perished in the general world's unrest over the next year or so.

I won't go into the details mainly because really, I don't know too many of the details. From what I understand, there are very few people left that do understand the details anymore anyhow. All I was taught in history class is that after the great upheaval, there were other countries in the world that sought to gain the top dog position that Amerca used to have and so they brought out and used their old 'weapons of mad destruction' on each other. From what I remember learning in class is that the Ruskers and Chinos were the first, but then when other states heard about their bombs being exploded, they also jumped in to try and maybe become the top dog. The Izzers bombed the Ruskers; the Chinos bombed the Ruskers and Injers; the Injers bombed the Chinos and Ruskers; the Urdus bombed the Izzers; the Frankers bombed the Russkers, and so on in addition to most of them jumping in against Amerca. From what I understand, there just wasn't that much left of the old world after everyone got done with taking care of old grudges. But that was a long, long time ago.

People tell me I wander around quite a bit when I talk so I need to get back to what happened to me at the camp.

I signed up for the annual ten-day workshop after being picked as eligible when I realized that I had to learn those skills to live on my own, if necessary, instead of being just another person in the village of Sultanawash that does the odd things like keep the store, work in the clothing factory, sweep the streets, and most loathsome of all, teach in the local school. There were three people from our class that didn't get approved to go out there; Majerston because he is a basic wimp that is always sick and who needs that kind of person out in the wilderness anyway; Rajenee because she is smarter than all get-out and the village knows that sooner or later she'll be elected mayor to replace Mr. Joniak so why take a chance at her getting injured; and finally Rasmun who has problems tying his shoelaces and who needs a lump like him wandering around out there. We need either the training class completion or the approval of the town when we hit our twenty-first birthday in order to legally take one of our parent's last names and also to be able to marry. And then the culmination of it all is when we reach our thirtieth birthday when we will finally be able to be addressed as Mister or Missus. I thought it would be a good thing to take this class because first of all, I'll be able to earn my living doing what I want to do, as well as be able to keep myself fed on a regular basis, and secondly, in order to be a voting member of the town once I hit twenty-one.

Hunting and foraging are necessary skills because we're so secluded up here that big shipments from Micoazonon only come in about once every six days or so; the deliveries that come in daily are just small stuff. That one salesperson from Micoazonon that visited about two or three years ago tried to get everyone hooked up with their new quick-order system where all you have to do is put on the helmet and think about what you wanted and zippo, within a couple hours this little flying thing comes buzzing in and drops off your package. Everybody was really impressed by the helmets and most everyone signed up with the salesman but a day later when a couple drone things came by and dropped off a full-size apple tree in old Mrs. Jeronas' front yard, most everyone turned off and turned in their helmets. Evidently, the old lady forgot she was wearing her helmet and got a sudden taste for an apple and zippo, the apple tree got delivered. Of course, she didn't have enough dollars to pay for it so the drone things latched onto one of her pet goats as payment and flew away.

And to cap off the problem with the helmets, shortly after the apple tree episode was the case of young Hardly Seasalt who found the helmet that his parents had stashed in the attic after vowing to never use it. Later that afternoon, zippo here came the drone things again and this time they dropped off a very sedated, very attractive, naked young woman in the Seasalt front yard. Evidently, Hardly was a bit underwhelmed by the quality of the girls in town and getting a girlfriend took over his thoughts. The girl, we never did find out her name, got taken back by the drone things to wherever she came from when Hardly's parents refused delivery. They could legally do that because Hardly was only twelve at the time, not fourteen which was the minimum age Micoazonon allows for a legit order.

As a result of that experience, that very evening there was a town meeting and it was decided that everyone should turn in their helmets to Mr. Bacon, the town sheriff, to lock them up somewhere where nobody could find them, and that only in an emergency was Mr. Bacon to allow anyone to use one again. They first tried contacting the Micoazonon salesman but he refused to come out, so locking the helmets up was the only other option. Funny, but after the salesman was contacted about the affair with Hardly, all our helmets flashed red and when Mr. Bacon put one on to find out what was going on, the helmet just said "software update in progress, please wait" for about an hour or two, but afterwards when one of the older boys tried requesting his own naked girl, the helmet kept saying "invalid request, please try again". Anyway, what we all used to do when someone wanted anything special, that is, not readily available here, they'd make their list and give it to Mr. Jorim who is the town courier. He used to get on his old black and white horse and do the journey to Norbendwash, a round trip of about four or five days to the Micoazonon outlet factory and almost always the drones would bring what we wanted within a day or two. Now, it seems like it must be every day one of those things comes to drop something off after the Micoazonon salesperson convinced Mr. Joniak to install that order console thing in the town hall. I've been told Norbendwash is a goofy little town made up mainly of people that work for Micoazonon, which means they're all in a real big hurry all the time. I really wouldn't like to be picked to take over Mr. Jorim's job if he ever gets hurt or too old to do it anymore.

Anyway, I'm wandering again, so let me try to get back to my story.

Here we were, all twelve of us, out in the dense woods at least a day's ride north of town. Well, at least I think it was north of town but I can't be absolutely sure because they blindfolded everyone after we got on the carts. Then they hitched up the horses and off we went, only stopping for a pee break about halfway there. They try to set the pace of the horses so that they get to the campsite just about mid-day so there's light enough to unload everyone and their supplies but no real sun position is available to really tell where the camp is, and then give enough time for the carts to get back to Sultanawash. For all I know, the camp could be just an hour's ride from town, but I'm probably wrong. After they dumped us all off, the drivers turned around and headed back to town. See, we don't have any of those soobroo-things in our town. After all, what do we need them for anyway? Sultanawash is right on a cliff overlooking the great Sealth Bay which stretches dozens of miles north and south of us. The bay is only maybe about two hundred feet deep at most over the whole expanse but it just goes on and on almost from horizon to horizon. We were taught that Old Sultanawash was actually sitting down about two or three miles off the cliff we're on, but when the Great Upheaval came, the town was relocated up a couple hundred feet onto the cliff we're on now. On clear days, one can look out across the water and see little islets dotting here and there where they say there used to be other towns long ago.

So, we really don't need much more than the horses and donkeys we have and breed, and our boats which we use to go fishing in the bay. The nearest village is Skykowash, about a day's ride east, but there's not much there other than about a hundred people living on the bank of the river doing fishing and not a whole lot else. I don't think they have a food store like we do so I really don't know how they manage to live. Every now and then, someone from there will make the trip down to us to trade some deerskins for some seeds, but we haven't seen anyone from there in about five months or so, so who knows if they are still living or not?

Okay, enough rambling; back to the story of "what happened".

We had moved all of our stuff into the big log cabin at camp and then our teacher, Mr. Jivey, brought out that evening's dinner for us all. We sat around the central firepit with the roaring fire he built toasting up pieces of bay carp and seed cakes and potatoes and carrots, all just having a good time. We were almost done when Mr. Jivey stood up and gave his opening speech.

"Welcome campers to this year's Wilderness class. You've all been selected to be here so you should feel at least somewhat appreciated by the great town of Sultanawash." Mr. Jivey had lived in town for all of his thirty-six years and was fully indoctrinated in the job he had to do with us. He was usually a pretty-fair-minded person that would give other people time to say what they wanted to say before he said anything. He was also pretty smart and had been the chief teacher at the Sultanawash school for the past twelve or so years, long enough for him to learn the old teaching manuals pretty much backward and forward. One thing he wasn't was inquisitive; he'd rather just go along with the way things were and not make anyone unhappy by asking questions like "and why do you think that way?" No, he'd take people at face-value and if they said one thing and did another, he'd put it down to them being forgetful rather than the other person being untruthful which doesn't happen much anyway.

"I'm going to show you the different methods of hunting and gathering food, whether hunting animals or gathering fresh fruit and vegetables. You are going to have to learn these skills in order to have a better chance of surviving in this world of ours. I'm also going to show you some basic medical skills because I'm sure sooner or later one of you is going to hurt themselves. This meal you've just eaten is the last of the food that came with us so from now on, if you want to eat anything, you'd better pay attention to what I say" as he glared at Glukey sitting next to me who was busy staring across the firepit at Amber, the girl of his dreams. I caught Mr. Jivey's stare and nudged Glukey back to the present.

"Alright then," Mr. Jivey continued as he hitched up his pants yet again, "the first thing we have to learn is proper fire management. You all pretty much know how to build and start a fire, but how many of you know the proper way to put one out?"

"I do, I do" Sansa piped up as she raised her hand. She was always doing that in school and it drove most people a bit nutso. We all supposed that it had something to do with her mother and father and how smitten they were with each other, to the point where it almost appeared that they forgot that they had a daughter. If we were in class and the teacher asked a question, Sansa could almost always be counted on to be the first to raise her hand. What couldn't be counted on was that Sansa would have the correct answer.

"First you separate the burning logs or sticks, then throw water on them, then bury the sticks and coals under a couple inches of sand or dirt. Right?" asked Sansa.

"That's the initial steps, thank you Sansa" said Mr. Jivey with a bit of a grimace, as if just the sound of Sansa's voice was painful to hear, which it sometimes was.

"After those steps are taken, one must always monitor the buried fire to ensure that it hasn't ignited some of the vegetable matter in the soil that it is buried under…"

"Didn't you take the vegetables out of the fire?" interrupted Dorman as he seemingly woke out of his usual trance-like state.

"No son, I'm just saying that if there is material like old leaves, peat moss, or whatever in with the dirt you're trying to bury the fire with, it could be ignited and smolder for quite some time after you think the fire has gone out. In which case, all you need is a bit of a breeze to spread some of that smoldering material into the rest of the forest and the whole forest could go up in flames."

"Oh, I thought you meant that you hadn't taken the vegetables out of the fire where they were roasting for tonight's dinner" said Dorman with that same old idiotic look on his face. Dorman isn't the brightest star in the heavens by a long shot, but at least if you tell him to go do something he'll do it, and surprisingly enough, he'll do a pretty fair job of whatever it is. He is really good with his hands but thinking just isn't his long suit.

"Alright then" said Mr. Jivey in that "why do I always volunteer for this job" voice that I was able to catch every now and then when he was trying to get certain difficult to understand points across in class. "By my watch it is now about nine-thirty and I want all of you to take care of your bodily functions over in that bath shed over there, then go to the cabin, unpack your stuff, get in your bed, and go to sleep. Tomorrow morning, I am going to wake you up at about six o'clock and we will get started at that time with your first lesson in gathering food for breakfast. So, get everything taken care of and get to bed."

"Oh, boys sleep on the right-hand side of the cabin, girls sleep on the left-hand side. And if I catch a boy or girl on the wrong side at any time during the night, you will get sent back to town immediately and will have to explain to Mrs. DeAngelo just what happened and why you were out of place. Furthermore, if any rules are broken over the next ten days here, whoever breaks them will be treated exactly the same, meaning having to explain to Mrs. DeAngelo."

Mrs. DeAngelo is the town minister and is notorious for being meaner than all get-out if "the rules between boys and girls" are broken, or if they are even bent just a little. She is pretty fair and even-handed, meaning she'll use that old cane of hers on girl-butts just as vigorously as on boy-butts. Also, once a person gets on her bad side, they stay there for a good long time. She had been appointed minister about twenty years ago by the old minister, Mr. Howdah, when he got sick from the lesionaires-14 disease and knew that that was pretty much a death sentence. Prior to becoming minister, Mrs. DeAngelo had been a teacher at the school and notorious for teaching exactly what each of the manuals said. She didn't take any back-talk from anyone when she was teaching so Mr. Howdah had thought she was a natural for being the new minister and keeping us all on the straight and narrow path to redemption when we die.

Anyway, that's where things sat after we arrived for our first night out at The Wilderness Camp. Little did any of us expect what was going to happen next.

Chapter 2 – *That Awful Next Morning*

It just occurred to me that I've never introduced myself, but of course it feels funny to introduce myself in my own journal. My name is Eaglefeeder and I'm seventeen years old. Most people just call me EG because it's easier to pronounce, especially with so many people having that lip disease which makes pronouncing 'F' a little difficult so my name usually comes out something like "Eaglefweedah". My parents are Raindrum and Hyacinth Whitehorse and they work at the barter-house grocery store measuring and weighing all the produce, fruits, and meat parts that people bring in. The good stuff they sort out, freeze, and then they call Micoazonon for a pickup and that's how we all make dollars. The lower-class stuff, like the blueberries that are too ripe to ship, we keep in town and people buy and sell them like normal. But it's not like we're some hick town that only has small farms; the town's main business is the clothing factory where we make all kinds of woolen clothes from the sheep and mountain goats most people keep and we then ship out a big pile of clothing every two or three weeks which is the town's main source of income. We also have a fully functional medical clinic that helps people when they hurt themselves, but old Doctor Yoronuki is getting on in years so there's been some discussion on who is going to replace him.

I've never really seen a dollar in my life but my parents tell me it's all kept electronically in our account with Micoazonon, which seems odd because the only things we actually have that are electronic are stuff like light bulbs, refrigerators, and farming equipment, so how can our dollars be electronic? I asked my parents once about that and they weren't really sure themselves but said as long as it works, that's all that counts.

With all the mentions about Micoazonon, I guess I should explain what they do. Like I said before, one of their so-called 'distribution centers' is in the town of Norbendwash about forty miles away. I asked Mr. Jorim about it once and he told me it's a huge set of buildings covering much more area than our town, and there are just hordes of people always running around from building-to-building grabbing boxes of this and that and feeding them into the drone-loading building. He said it's amazing to watch because a drone flies out of that building and disappears into the sky every couple seconds all day long both sending out packages to customers and receiving packages from suppliers. I told him that there must be a whole lot of little towns like ours around here to keep that place so busy and Mr. Jorim said that wasn't the only Micoazonon place around. He said he's heard that there are literally thousands of these places in the lands to the east of us across the mountains as well as south of us. It just boggles the mind how they keep all those orders straight is what I replied and he told me that a long, long time ago it actually was two huge companies, one that made the instructions that the drones run on and the other that did all the shipping and that after the big upheaval, they naturally just combined and decided to rebuild the world through buying and selling all kinds of stuff to keep everyone happy and alive. I have to say that without Micoazonon, we'd be living quite differently and without some of the luxuries we have like those genuine mattresses and the food blenders. I vaguely remember one of the generators going out when I was a little kid and it being a whole day before Micoazonon could get us a new one, so I guess they are doing a good job of at least keeping towns like ours stable and maybe even making some progress with making life easier for all involved. Now, we have these big wind turbine things arrayed on the hills about a mile or so to the east and they supply just about all the electricity we can use; the generators are only needed when we hang all the lights out for the Exmas festival at the end of the year. The whole town chipped in to buy those wind generators about ten or so years ago, and boy, I have to say those things work just great.

All these random thoughts are just clouding the issue again, so let me get back to that first day at camp and go through what happened.

So, we all went into the cabin to get ready for bed that first night, girls on the left and boys on the right of the big divider curtain hung right down the middle. I was able to snag a bed about halfway between the front and back doors so I knew I wasn't going to have people running past my bed during the night going to the outside bathroom. Glukey got the bed next to mine while his sister Sukey got the bed opposite. Amber managed to get the bed on the far end of the girl's side, then there was Sukey, Josanna, Wassa, Elnor, Aku, Sansa, and Jellie. On our side was Dorman, Glukey, me, and

Timtim. Mr. Jivey had his own curtained off area at the far end next to the back door. So, that was the sleeping arrangement for all thirteen of us; eight girls, four boys, and Mr. Jivey.

Glukey Railsford is my best friend and he is about eight months older than me. His sister Sukey is about four months younger than me and for a while I was spending free time with Sukey but she didn't really seem to care for me a whole lot, I mean I would start talking to her and she would pretty much clam up or sputter and stammer and turn really red in the face, so I dropped any type of serious talking with her and just kept her as a friend. Their younger sister, Lackey, is a whole different matter. She will butt in all the time when I'll be trying to talk to Sukey or hang out with Glukey and just makes a royal pain of herself. It is very good that she is two grades behind us so we didn't have to put up with her, for once. I also have to mention that their parents are a bit odd which shows up in their kids' names. The story is that their mother wanted to have children that were sweet and adorable, so after asking Micoazonon since it also stores a lot of information besides real things, she found alternate names for 'sugar' and so insisted on naming her children Glucose, Sucrose, and Lactose, but those names just really sounded horrible so we all shortened them. Lackey still gets a bit peeved if someone calls her Lactose, but the other two pretty much shrug it all off. I remember that one time when Lackey was out with Glukey, Sukey, and me one evening and Mrs. Railsford, their mama, called out from their back door "Lac-TOSE! It's your bedtime" and we all got a good snicker out of that one. Well, not Lackey for sure. And after that, Sukey started calling her either 'Lick Toes' or 'Lock

Toes' which is another reason Lackey doesn't like her full name.

It was a while after everyone got in their beds for the night, there was some snoring coming from TimTim so I knew he was asleep, but I could tell that Glukey wasn't asleep just yet. I whispered "hey, what are you thinking about?" but got no response so I just rolled over and tried to sleep. Just a bit later as I was falling asleep, I heard very faint footsteps from the far end of the girl's side which caused my eyes to open up a bit. I cautiously looked around in the dim moonlight but nothing caught my eye until I saw a shape peeking around the curtain. It looked like Amber in her pj's and sure enough, when I concentrated, I could see her beckoning with her finger to me. I was about to get up when I heard Glukey stirring in his bed, then cautiously get out of it. I silently watched as he slowly tiptoed down the aisle to where Amber was, then they both reached out and grasped each other's hand.

Nobody was prepared when an alarm bell started ringing quite loudly, all the lights flashed on, and Mr. Jivey came stumbling and hurrying down the aisle. By the time he reached Glukey and Amber, everyone else was wide awake and yelling all sorts of things; Aku was whimpering and white as a ghost, Josanna and Wassa were both red in the face like they'd been caught doing something, Elnor was barking about having her sleep ruined, Sukey was staring at Glukey and Amber with a mean look on her face, and so on. Mr. Jivey had a small square box in his hand and as he got to the two of them, he squeezed it and the alarm stopped.

"I TOLD you", he shouted, "that nobody was allowed on the wrong side of the cabin. In the morning, I'm sending both of you back to report to Mrs. DeAngelo for breaking the rules. What have you got to say for yourselves?"

"Uh uh uh" sputtered Glukey, living up to his reputation for not being very quick on answering when caught doing something he shouldn't be doing.

"I was, uh, just, uh, uh, you know, uh, going to the bathroom. That's it, I was going to the bathroom and I guess I just happened to be going at the same time Glukey was, so I bumped into him" answered Amber, always a bit quicker with excuses.

"Uh, yeah, I had to go something fierce and wasn't looking where I was going and ran into Amber" said Glukey hoping that this might pass as a reasonable excuse. "I mean, I *had* to go, look, you can see where I peed myself when the alarm went off" he said as he pointed down. Yep, there was a slight wet spot on the front of his nightshirt, but I think he was just drooling again like he usually did when talking to or about Amber.

"Yeah well, I don't know if I'm going to believe you or not. But let this be a lesson to you two, and to all the rest of you also. When I said no crossing over to the other side, I meant it, and as you now know, I have taken precautions so that anyone who does immediately sets off the alarm. Now, I'm tired and want to go back to sleep. We got an early day tomorrow and we all need some rest, so GET BACK IN YOUR BEDS AND STAY THERE!". Mr. Jivey then turned and stomped back to his curtained off little cubbyhole and we could all hear the bedsprings squeak as he got back in his bed.

We all got back in our beds and tried not to think of what other little tricks or alarms Mr. Jivey might have in store for us until we all fell asleep for the remainder of the night.

* * *

"WAKEY WAKEY! WAKE UP YOU LITTLE DARLINGS! GET YOUR BUTTS OUT OF THOSE BEDS AND GET DRESSED!" was the next thing all of us heard. Mr. Jivey was stomping up and down the aisle pulling the curtain open and yelling for us to get moving. Everyone was groaning a bit as they got out of bed, all except Amber. She was just lying there in her bed not moving so Mr. Jivey stomped down to her bed and yelled once more "GET UP AND OUT OF YOUR BED RIGHT NOW!". But Amber still didn't move one bit. Mr. Jivey shouted "AMBER!" as he reached down and shook her shoulder but she still didn't move. All the rest of us stopped what we were doing and watched as he slowly rolled Amber over and we all saw the big red gash across her neck; the once-white pillow was now stained dark red. Her lifeless eyes were open and staring at the ceiling as Mr. Jivey quickly ran out the door. We could all hear him throwing up for a few seconds and then he slowly walked back in; all the color had drained out of his face even though he was sweating to beat the band; he looked entirely lost. He stopped at Amber's bed and his mouth opened but nothing came out. All the rest of us were moving in slo-mo as we slowly crept to her bed to look at her. None of us to my knowledge had ever seen a dead person before so it was both enticing as a novelty, but also repulsive in that we all knew her and now she'd never be around anymore.

We all looked at one another trying to figure out who did it but everyone looked the same; very pale faces with similar expressions of "what the heck happened?".

Chapter 3 – *What Happened After the First Murder*

I want to give you some background. Sultanawash was, up to that point at least, a very peaceful place. We never really had any problems, heck, Mr. Bacon was the town sheriff but the most he ever had to do was lock up old Amboy every now and then when Amboy hit the moonshine a bit too heavy. The last time, Amboy had just brewed a new batch and after very evidently taste-testing a decent portion, he started throwing rocks at Mrs. Herula's dog, so Mr. Bacon grabbed him and took him off to the jail to sleep it off. Everyone feared having to go to jail, partly because of the social stigma, but also because it was a run-down old shack that used to be used as a pigsty and as a result stank to high-heaven inside, but then all the pigs died from that blistery disease so when we got some more, we made sure to keep them in a different place. But outside of that time, I think the only other person in the last year or so that got put in there for a night was one of those stump-jumpers that come wandering through here every now and then. You can always tell one of those people that wander around the wilderness and don't really live in a town because they all have those little sores on their faces and hands. Anyway, that guy had been told by someone, who had heard something from someone else, that we had a booming town here with lots of single girls that wanted to get married.

Well, after he tried hugging and kissing Sukey - she is pretty good looking - when he saw her walking down the street to the store, Mr. Bacon grabbed him and tossed him in jail for the night. The next morning, Mr. Bacon let the man out and let him know that if he didn't leave town at once and never come back, he'd spend at least a month in the jail. The guy first started yelling derogatory names at Mr. Bacon like 'gas-guzzler' and 'bugger-snout' but then took one more look at the jail and took off southward; we never did see him again. I think also part of his decision to leave was based on the fact that during the struggle with Sukey, she managed to knee him pretty hard in the privates, which was what put him on the ground and allowed Mr. Bacon to haul him off. After all, why would a guy want to marry a girl that gave him the knee anyway?

So, there we all were, staring at Amber's dead body when finally, Sukey says "now what do we do?".

That kinda shook everyone out of their daze and Mr. Jivey said "OK, first off everyone change out of your pj's and then Jellie and Aku, you go get one of those old tarps that are in the shed out back of the cabin. Dorman, I want you to go out and find two long straight branches about as thick as your wrist and about as tall as you are." You had to give Dorman explicit instructions otherwise he'd come back with a whole tree. "Sansa, you pick up Amber's stuff and put it all back in her backpack. The rest of you, well, you go back and sit on your bunks."

"How are we going to get back to town? The carts and horses are gone and we can't call them back. What are we gonna do?" spluttered Timtim, never the bravest one around.

"That's just it, we can't get back to town. They won't send the carts and horses back for another nine days" replied Mr. Jivey.

"Well, you know where we are, don't you? How long is it if we just walked back to town?" asked Elnor, always the practical one.

"I'm afraid it's a good twelve to fourteen-hour walk back to town, so what we're going to do is just put Amber's body someplace safe and cold and just wait for the carts to come back. After all, I'm the only one who knows the way back but I'm also the only one that has the skills to be able to live out here without supplies, remember, this is supposed to be a training class in how to survive. So, since I'm the only one who knows how to live out here, I can't leave the rest of you to fend for yourselves because you'd be starving in no time. Either that, or you'd eat something poisonous or hurt yourself trying to hunt, and then where would you all be? So, since I have to stay with you, and it's way too long a walk, we all stay here until the carts and horses come back to pick us up."

"Mr. Jivey?" I interrupted.

"Yes?"

"Why didn't the alarm go off?"

Mr. Jivey stood there for a second or two as he thought about my question, then said "To tell the truth, I was so tired that I don't remember setting it again after Glukey and Amber set it off that once." For all Mr. Jivey was the school's chief teacher, at times he surprised me with how slow he really thought; maybe it was because he didn't learn anything but just memorized it all? Oh well, thoughts for another day and time. But after he said he didn't remember setting the alarm again, Glukey turned and stared at Mr. Jivey with a very unkind look on his face, as if to say "Me and Amber could have at least had one more conversation together if we knew that!"

It was Elnor who blurted out what I'm sure all of us were thinking "So it could have been any one of us that killed Amber". Elnor was more often than not a fairly bossy type girl; a person who often rubbed people the wrong way, as opposed to Jellie who knew how to rub you the right way, if you know what I mean. Elnor was eighteen and used to running her house since her mother had died about ten years ago. Elnor's father missed her mother something fierce and got really down in the dumps for a while so Elnor was faced with the task of keeping that family going. Over the years, her added responsibilities had turned her from a nice young girl into a woman who was used to setting the rules and that's that. Where once she was a little on the chubby side as a girl, she was now thin and tall, and had what appeared to be a perpetual frown on her face. I'm sure she knew a lot about how to survive but was in this class in order to be certified as having the life skills necessary in order to start her own family. The problem was that there were few boys in town that wanted to even get to know her better since she always seemed to be in a hurry because there was always so much to do. I was actually amazed that she could run her household, take care of her two younger sisters and her father, and go to school at the same time. I could only guess that she was a *very* determined person.

Sansa broke the trance that ensued after Elnor's comment with "How can you say that? Anybody could have come in here during the night since none of the doors were locked. It could have been another one of those stump-jumpers or some wild animal; how are we supposed to know?"

"Alright, quiet down everyone. We'll take care of Amber first and then after we have the memorial cleansing, we'll look into it. But first…" Mr. Jivey was saying as Dorman came hustling back into the cabin with two long tree branches. Right after that, Aku and Jellie walked in lugging the folded tarp.

"Ok, spread that tarp out on the floor next to Amber's bed" Mr. Jivey then said. "And, you, Dorman, help me lift Amber off the bed and put her in the middle of the tarp."

After Aku and Jellie unfolded the tarp, Mr. Jivey stood at the foot of the bed and Dorman the head. "Ok, reach under her and grab her shoulders, then lift" as Mr. Jivey grabbed Amber's ankles. They both lifted Amber's body off the bed and then shuffled over to where the tarp was and set her down. Mr. Jivey then rolled over the edges of the tarp to cover Amber's body and asked Dorman to put his poles down on the edges. Mr. Jivey then tied the four corners of the tarp to the poles and asked Dorman to help him carry the makeshift stretcher outside.

As soon as Mr. Jivey and Dorman walked out with Amber, Sukey turned to Glukey and said sternly "So what happened between you two?"

"Hey, I didn't do anything. After that thing with the alarm and lights last night, I crawled back in my bed and stayed there the whole night. It wasn't me!" Glukey protested.

"Well, you were the one who was always trying something with Amber" Sukey retorted.

"Exactly, so why would I want to harm Amber?" Glukey protested further.

"Hey, hey, I don't think this is the time or the place to start with that" I butted in.

"Oh yeah? And why would you want to stop any speculations if you weren't feeling guilty?" snapped Elnor.

"Guilty of what? I didn't get out of my bed at all last night except when the alarm sounded" I protested since Elnor put the spotlight on me. "And who says it was one of us? You girls are also just as much suspects as us boys are" I sputtered lamely.

Josanna took that occasion to put in her contribution "Oh yeah? What girl would do something like that?" Josanna never did have many original thoughts that passed through her head and was more than agreeable to joining the popular opinions just so she would fit in. She isn't a particularly bad person, looks pretty nice, tall, nice legs, short blond hair, but sometimes she would behave just like the sheep and goats Mrs. Herula kept, that is, whichever way the wind blew or whatever someone else said, she'd go that direction or echo whatever someone else said. Wassa was her best friend and they were like two peas in a pod; they dressed alike, talked alike, had their hair cut the same way, and of course, thought so much alike one would have thought they were twins.

"And why is it that a girl wouldn't be capable of that since you are also here to learn life skills?" was my scintillating come-back.

"Because none of us would ever think of doing that" Wassa said snottily.

"Oh yeah?" was another less-than-brilliant reply from my lips.

"Hey, hey, like we're getting ahead of ourselves" broke in Sansa, "there's absolutely no reason why it couldn't have been someone else who came in here during the night. I mean, Amber's bed was right next to the door and who knows, maybe someone came in here and Amber woke up and that person then killed her?"

"Yeah, that sounds a bit far-fetched to me" Elnor said warily.

Just then Mr. Jivey and Dorman came back in.

"What's going on? I told you we were going to do the memorial cleansing rite after we took care of Amber" Mr. Jivey said.

"We were just…" started Sansa but Glukey butted in with "The girls were accusing one of us boys with killing Amber and…"

Mr. Jivey stopped that firmly with "I don't want to hear any of that talk around here, at least not just yet. We have a dead friend that has left us forever and we need to go through the memorial cleansing first before we can start…"

It was meek little Aku that broke in with what all of us, save one, were thinking at that point in time "Geezo-peezo, but what if it happens again?"

Chapter 4 - *Another One Bites the Dust*

I remember there was a long pause in all the talking as Aku's words sunk in; even Mr. Jivey had a look of terror cross his face momentarily. Aku is a genuinely nice person even though she had a face that resembled her father more than her mother, and that wasn't a compliment. She was rather short, like her mother, had dark hair like her mother, and was a bit cross-eyed like her mother. After those comparisons, all the rest of her features took after her father. She had bony cheeks, a prominent chin with a big dimple in the middle, and quite bushy eyebrows. If you looked closely and the light was right, you could actually see wisps of her father's mustache to top it all off. But like I say, she is a truly nice person to be around, thoughtful, calm, and very sincere in all that she says and does.

"Uh well, we'll get to that after we go through the memorial cleansing, so right now we need to all calm down a bit and get our minds aligned so we can do the ceremony" Mr. Jivey finally said. "I'll expect everyone to be out at the campfire pit in ten minutes, so you'd better all go sit on your bunks and prepare for the ceremony."

To recap what the memorial cleansing ceremony is, since I don't know for sure whether or not other towns do it or not, it's where the members of our community that choose to participate come together after a person dies, though most people participate. There was that one time when old Mr. Jagdiz died and since he could be such a cranky guy at times, only about ten or so people showed up at his ceremony. Contrast that with when Mr. Herula died and since he was such an all-around nice guy, there must have been at least two-hundred people for his ceremony.

But back to what the ceremony actually is. We all prepare ourselves mentally beforehand by doing our calming exercises and by that, I mean sitting, closing our eyes, and mentally reviewing any and all experiences with the dead person. When we are all prepared, usually no more than about ten- or fifteen-minutes' worth, we all sit around in a circle, hold hands, then concentrate on sharing our minds with everyone else. It was important that the ceremony be performed within the first day, otherwise the memories wouldn't be fresh enough to share. It was a shame that Amber's parents couldn't be here to share and participate but that's the rules.

We all sat and concentrated for a bit and then Mr. Jivey led us out in a solemn line to the firepit. We all sat down on the stone benches there, looked at each other, then interlocked our hands with the people sitting next to us on each side so we formed a continuous chain around the campfire. Mr. Jivey, seated two spots over from me, then said in a loud calm voice "We are here to share Amber, what we thought, what we saw, and how we felt about her. It is our way of remembering the dead and assisting them on their way to the hereafter since our thoughts and feelings will accompany her on her way. Thus, armed with the good wishes of her friends, she will be assured of a comfortable transition to the next world. Now let us all close our eyes and let Amber fill our minds by sharing our memories."

Then he looked around and when he was satisfied that everyone was prepared, he closed his eyes and started the chant to lead us and link us.

"Lord of all, we ask your guidance and pray that you accept Amber into your arms. Lead us, guide us, remember. Lead us. Guide us. Remember."

We all joined in the chant at that point and I felt my mind opening to those around me. I couldn't pick out any specific person's thoughts but I started seeing Amber from the perspective of the other people there. I could guess that the images of Amber that showed how beautiful she was came from Glukey, but didn't have a clue as to where or from whom the other images came. That memory of her laughing at a joke with that twisted little smile of hers probably came from Jellie, and so on. My memories of Amber included the time she helped me with some homework and that time that she hit me with a water balloon at the annual summer harvest fest we have. As soon as those memories came and went, there were others that floated through my mind; some of them were mine but I'm guessing most were from the others in the circle. After a time, it could have been two minutes or twenty, it felt almost as if Amber were with us again; that was the power of our ceremony. With so many memories of the person, they almost come alive again in the flesh instead of just in our memories.

Suddenly, the ceremony twisted and a pain sliced through my neck as I saw a fleeting image of Amber's horror-stricken face as a knife with a wooden handle glided its way through the soft flesh of her neck. As her blood splashed up, the memory sharing abruptly ended and we all broke the circle.

I looked around and evidently everyone else had seen the same thing since most of them were holding their heads in pain. Aku was crying, as were Josanna, Wassa, and Dorman. Both Sukey and Sansa looked as white as a ghost and Elnor's eyes were wide open to match her mouth as she gasped for air. As I looked around, Jellie evidently fainted since she had slid off her bench. Timtim looked like nothing I had ever seen before with a combination of fear and hatred on his face. Glukey's face was stark white but his mouth was twisted into a snarl.

"Who did it? WHICH ONE OF YOU DID IT?" he screamed. "We all saw it happen so that means it was one of you, so who's going to own up to it? I swear right now, I WILL FIND OUT WHO DID IT AND YOU WILL PAY FOR WHAT YOU DID!!!"

Mr. Jivey finally came back out of his trance, stood, and grabbed Glukey by the arm. "Calm down; we'll find out who did it but I can't allow you to go off by yourself because that will make you no better than the one who did do it, so calm down. PLEASE calm down, all of you."

* * *

I think it was about an hour or so later that we all assembled again around the firepit. After that horrific image of Amber's throat being slashed, Mr. Jivey herded all of us back into the cabin and had us all lie down on our cots. I don't know about the others, but I sure needed that rest to get rid of the feeling of that knife slicing through and to get my mind back into my own body. I'm not kidding when I say that seeing that image made me actually feel at least some of what Amber had felt; that was the power of the memory sharing, even though Amber wasn't really an active part. Our collective memories had combined to bring her back to life in our minds and her pain reached back across the line between life and death.

"Ok, we all saw the murder through the murderer's eyes, so that means that one of us is the murderer. So, who wants to admit to it?" Mr. Jivey asked.

Total silence enveloped us all as we all looked around at each other; evidently nobody was willing to confess.

"Alright then, we're going to have to figure out who did it and why. Can anyone think of a reason why Amber of all people should have been killed? Anyone?" Mr. Jivey asked as he looked around with a hopeful look.

Dead silence reigned again.

Finally, Sansa, evidently nervous with silence that she was always accustomed to filling with words, spoke with a quaver in her voice "Um, I thought Amber was really nice and I can't think of any reason why someone would kill her."

Glukey coughed once and then spat out "Amber never harmed anyone, never had a bad word to say about anyone, and was just really nice, so why did one of you do it? Just for kicks? Why? Please say something." When we all sat there with blank looks on our faces, he added in "You're all about as useless as hair grease."

"Ok, just hold your horses on accusing anyone," said Mr. Jivey. "First off, we're going to go down the row of beds and I'm going to ask everyone what they heard or saw through the night."

"Well, I didn't see…" started Sansa, always trying to be first.

Mr. Jivey cut her off by barking "I SAID WE'D GO DOWN THE ROW OF BEDS. NOW, WHAT ABOUT THAT DIDN'T GET THROUGH YOUR THICK HEAD???"

Sansa immediately wilted into the background, so Mr. Jivey continued with "I think the best way for me to go about this is to take each of you one by one and go through it, ok? Let's see, Jellie, you were in the bed closest to Amber, so let's go out back a-ways and we can talk." He stood up as did Jellie and they both walked around the back of the cabin.

Elnor took that opportunity to fill the responsibility vacuum and said sternly "I don't care what he thinks and does. I want to know which one of you did it? C'mon now, fess up."

The rest of us immediately started babbling various things such as "Who died and made you boss?", "I didn't hear or see anything", "Oh, just put a sack on it Elnor", "Leave me out of this", and so forth. Glukey was still looking like there was a storm raging inside him so I said "Hey, let's go for a walk" wanting to calm him down a bit. He looked at me, stopped frowning, and nodded, so we both got up and started ambling in the opposite direction of where Mr. Jivey and Jellie had gone.

* * *

It was about forty-five minutes later that I got interviewed by Mr. Jivey. We were sitting out on an old felled tree about a hundred feet from the cabin and the first thing he asked when I sat down was "Did you see or hear anything last night?"

I told him about seeing Amber beckoning to Glukey just as I was falling asleep, him getting out of his bed and walking over to her, then the alarm went off and all heck broke loose.

"But, after that. When everyone went back to their beds; did you see anything?" he asked earnestly. Evidently, he hadn't gotten any information from the others he had interviewed already and was still trying to figure it out.

"No, after everyone went back to bed, I just lay there for a while and then the next thing I knew you were waking us all up" I told him truthfully. "What I can't understand is why someone would do that to her. She was a nice person and pretty polite, so I just don't understand. Why would someone do that, Mr. Jivey? I mean, when was the last time someone in Sultanawash killed someone else? Why would they pick on Amber of all people?" I asked.

"As far as I know" Mr. Jivey started "the last time someone killed someone else was a long time ago. I vaguely remember my grandfather, Mr. Celiac, saying something about a stump-jumper coming to town when he was a boy and causing all kinds of problems and then one morning, he was found tied to that post in the center of town with a couple arrows through his chest; almost like someone was using him for target practice. Come to think of it, when I was a little kid there was a teenager that got expelled for drowning a cat. Hmmm…"

"Mr. Jivey?" I asked as he had this far-off look in his eyes.

"Yes?" he replied a moment later as he came back to here and now.

"Have you ever seen anyone with a knife like that? I mean, shouldn't we be looking for the knife and then maybe we can figure out who did it?"

"You know, that's a really good point" he replied as his lips firmed up. "I'm going to do just that; let's go back to the others."

So, we walked back to the cabin where the rest were lounging around or doing various things. Glukey and Sukey were sitting on a bench; she was holding his hand and occasionally nodding as he was slowly talking, most likely about Amber. Josanna and Wassa were talking while ambling around picking the odd wildflower every now and then. Timtim and Dorman were at the far end of the campsite splitting and stacking wood. Elnor was attempting to show Sansa the correct way to set up a fire in the firepit, while Aku was just sitting there staring into space.

"Ok everyone, gather around. I want all of you…" Mr. Jivey started to say but then abruptly stopped and asked "Where's Jellie?".

"She was just here" volunteered Sansa. "I think she may have gone to the bathroom."

"Ok, we'll wait a minute for her to get back. In the meantime, I want everyone to just stay here for a bit. I have to go into the cabin for a couple minutes and I don't want to be disturbed. Ok, so when Jellie gets back, you tell her I said to stay out here in a group, ok?" And then he turned and walked into the cabin.

"What's he doing?" asked Sukey in a low voice to me.

"I think he's looking for the knife" I replied in a loud whisper and was surprised when Sukey's face turned really white.

That set off everyone and they all started whispering various things like "I thought it was someone from outside", "He can't go through my stuff", "I hope he finds it so we don't have to be afraid anymore", and "Maybe he's got one of those phoney things and is calling the wagons back". A couple of us got up and started moseying around the firepit, kicking twigs and dirt, stomping on bugs, and talking about nothing in particular.

Ten minutes passed and Mr. Jivey finally came out of the cabin looking confused again.

"Well, did you find it?" asked Elnor.

"No, I didn't find anything. I don't know where else to look" Mr. Jivey answered.

Suddenly there was a shriek from the little bath house and we all looked over there. Sukey was in the doorway and she called out shakily "I found the knife".

Chapter 5 – *Oh No, Not Another One!*

We all got up hurriedly and ran over to the bath house. Sukey remained standing in the doorway looking like she had just seen a ghost.

Mr. Jivey barked "Everyone stay back; let me handle this" as he pushed aside Sukey. And of course, we all gathered in a bunch in the doorway trying to see what was going on. What we saw was Mr. Jivey standing there in the little aisleway between the shower stalls and the toilet cubicles. It took another moment to notice Jellie.

Jellie was sprawled out on the floor with that same look of terror that Amber had, but this was different. The haft of that same knife we'd all seen in Amber's memory ceremony was poking out of Jellie's chest while the blade it was attached to was buried deep in her.

Now, I liked Jellie. She was a little plump, a little short, but long on personality. She could find something good in just about every situation, good or bad. I remember the time she and I were picking tomatoes in her parent's garden and I tripped and fell face-first into a mud-puddle. I looked up at her expecting something sarcastic, like Josanna would have said "mud on your face does tend to make the rest of you look cleaner", or something disapproving like Elnor would probably have said “see what happens when you don’t watch where you’re walking”, but Jellie just said “the mud on your face really sets off the color of your red hair. You should do it more often.” It was almost as if Jellie had a different pair of eyes than everyone else; eyes that could see different colors or maybe just see things softer than what the rest of us saw. She was the one who started us all using the phrase “slow as a pumpkin”. When I asked her just what the heck that meant, she said “You ever see a pumpkin chase a cat?” and to this day I’m still not sure just what she was trying to say.

As we all continued to stare at Jellie lying there on the floor, Josanna dove into the silence and said “She was always a dreaming fool”. Even Wassa gasped at that callous remark. Now, I think I mentioned that Josanna and Wassa were like two peas in a pod; always saying similar things, dressing alike, and keeping more or less with each other for company. There were times when the two of them certainly earned their collective nickname which was, you guessed it, WassaJo. If one of them disagreed with something that was said or done, the other was sure to maintain that common front. If one of them decided to go swimming in the river, the other went also. It was like there was some kind of invisible rope that bound them together, heck, they even walked similarly with those long bouncing steps and wiggling their hips from side to side that Mrs. DeAngelo usually frowned on. But it was almost as if there was also an invisible cord or pipe that connected both their brains since, like I said, what one said, the other was sure to back up.

But this time, it was like Wassa all of a sudden realized she was a separate person with her own mind. Before anyone else could comment on Josanna's remark, Wassa barked right into Josanna's face "That was entirely uncalled for. Jellie was just a little simpler and more carefree than most; not like you that always puts on airs like you're so superior", and then she slapped Josanna across the face with her hand and finished with "you oomma-goomma dirtbag".

That gave everyone a shock since it was swearing to the nth degree, I mean the most I usually said was a 'holy catfish' every now and then because catfish are pretty rare around here. Anyway, we all expected Mr. Jivey to start yelling at Wassa but that wasn't quite what happened.

Josanna responded to being slapped by throwing a wicked right cross and landed her clenched fist right on the tip of Wassa's chin. Wassa momentarily stumbled but got right back into it with a hard left to Josanna's belly that put Josanna down on the ground outside the bathrooms gasping for air as she doubled over in pain. In the meantime, bossy Elnor tried to step in between them. Luckily for her, Sansa, showing some intelligence, pushed Elnor away just as Wassa aimed a kick at Josanna's face. Wassa missed Josanna but fell off-balance on top of Sansa who was trying to get out of the way. Elnor, mistaking Sansa's little shove, aimed a punch and clipped Sansa's right ear. Timtim tried helping Sansa and Wassa up but Wassa drilled her elbow into his gut and he went down while Elnor and Josanna were swinging at Wassa and Sansa again. Dorman, Glukey, and I were just standing there without a clue as to what to do, I mean fighting was definitely not allowed which was why this was such a bo-zo-no-no, when Mr. Jivey tried to separate everyone.

"What has gotten into you people?" Mr. Jivey panted as he finally managed to get everyone apart. Josanna was still holding her stomach in pain, Wassa had this look that could kill on her face, Sansa looked like a mess after Wassa and Timtim both fell on top of her, Timtim looked puzzled as usual, and the rest of us were just standing there wondering what they heck we should be doing. Glukey finally looked around and asked worriedly "Hey, where's Sukey?".

"Here I am" Sukey replied as she peered around the door to the bathrooms. She had this strange look on her face also, like watching Josanna and Wassa go at it was fun. I have to admit, I was a bit horrified at seeing the two girls punch it out, but there was also this other strange feeling I don't think I've ever had before, like watching the two girls and wondering who was going to win.

Let me say this - winning in our town was not something very celebrated. When we have the end of summer festival and everyone makes their special food dish so that we all sit down and pass them all around, there's no real "winner" as in who makes the best blueberry pie. Everyone just knows that Mrs. Herula makes these blueberry biscuit things, she calls them 'skawns', that are just so unbelievably tasty that literally nothing compares to it, so there really isn't a 'winner'. When we have the sack races and the three-legged races at the end there is no real winner, just a couple dozen people having a lot of fun. Jellie and I had an especially great time one year tied together for that race when she deliberately tripped me and then I felt her hands all over me and I mean ALL over me. And the other thing was, there are no real fights or arguments in our town; people take the good and the bad happenings as just something that, well, happens in life. So, seeing this little melee happen was something that was just unheard of.

"Hey" I said. "Where's Aku?"

Sansa immediately blanched white and with a tremble in her voice wailed "Oh noooo, not her too!"

"Timtim, Dorman, you two, go look for Aku. The rest of you, sit down and calm yourselves" Mr. Jivey commanded in a firm tone.

It was about a whole two minutes later that both of them came back with Aku. She was hanging on Dorman's shoulder crying her eyes out. Sure, Aku was what some called a sensitive girl, but I like to think she just cared more than others. But I don't think I ever saw her actually crying this much over anything before.

"What's the matter?" asked Mr. Jivey, but Aku just shook her head and then buried her face in Timtim's chest.

"What happened? Where did you find her?" Mr. Jivey asked Timtim.

Timtim paused for a moment to collect his thoughts, which from past experiences weren't many, and said "She was out back of the cabin when I found her. From what I could get out of her, she was just walking around trying to make sense of why someone would kill another person when she found a dead squirrel, and then lost it completely."

"A dead squirrel set her off?" asked Elnor contemptuously. "We got two dead people and she's all worked up about a squirrel? Who does she think she is, the Moaning Lisa?" She gave a snort, turned away, and started walking back towards the cabin, plainly fed up with Aku's bare emotions.

"Aku? What happened?" asked Mr. Jivey politely. "What did you see that made you so upset?"

Aku pulled her head out of Timtim's chest and whimpered "I was so sad about, about Amber and Jellie" she sniffed, "that I had to take a walk to try and, and figure it out. But then I saw it" and her face screwed up again and she turned back towards Timtim. After a second, she pulled out again and finished with "There was a squirrel lying there, oh lordy" and she started bawling again. Both Mr. Jivey and Timtim tried to calm her down but neither had any effect.

The rest of us were just standing there wondering what could upset Aku that much. It just didn't make any sense at all. But then, I thought about the group fight that had just happened and how that never happened before. Sure, people would get into disagreements occasionally but those were usually settled within a minute or two with one, or both, saying "I see your viewpoint" and walking away pondering just what the other person was trying to say. Raw emotions, that is, people hitting each other, yelling like Glukey had done earlier, and people crying their eyes out like Aku was now doing, just didn't happen.

It was like something had changed when we came out to the cabin, but just what that was I didn't have a clue.

Mr. Jivey interrupted my thoughts by saying in a loud voice that cracked a bit around the edges "Ok, we have to get through this. I want all of you to go to the cabin. To, The, Cabin, you hear me? Go to the cabin and prepare yourselves for the memorial cleansing ceremony for Jellie. I'll call you all out here in about twenty minutes. Go to the cabin and *stay there*."

We all moved off slowly, Josanna calling to Elnor who was off about fifty feet from the rest of us still gathered around Mr. Jivey. Glukey's face was still dark and stormy, Elnor looked extremely put-out, Sansa was still shaking a bit, Timtim was still holding onto Aku but at least she had stopped crying and was now just clinging with all her strength to Timtim; Josanna and Wassa were walking at least five feet apart but at least not throwing things at each other; Sukey looked odd but was walking steadily again; I saw the back of Dorman as he ambled off into the woods, and I followed them all while trying to think about what had happened and what was happening to us all. I tried but couldn't figure it out so just sat on my bed, closed my eyes, and started thinking about Jellie.

* * *

It must have been a good half-hour later when Mr. Jivey walked into the cabin and said "It's time that we all go out and remember…, hey, where's Dorman?"

Up to that point, we had all either been sitting or lying down on our beds quietly getting into the mood for Jellie's memorial ceremony, but at Mr. Jivey's words we all started looking around.

“Who saw him last?” barked Mr. Jivey as we were trying to clear our minds.

“The last I saw him, he was wandering around the firepit” said Sansa, always trying to get in the first, and last, word.

“Anyone see him come into the cabin?” asked Mr. Jivey, earnestly not wanting to hear about another body.

“No”, “I thought he was right behind me”, “I wasn’t paying attention”, and other comments came out as we all tried to get Jellie out of our minds and pay attention to the current situation.

“OKAY; everyone and I mean everyone, is to stay right where you are while I go out looking for Dorman. You understand? NOBODY LEAVES THEIR BED!” shouted Mr. Jivey, all the while sounding like he was on the verge of falling apart.

Chapter 6 – *That Horrible Vision*

Aku immediately burst into tears again while Timtim moved to her bed to console her again. They were swiftly becoming an item. What the rest of us weren't quite expecting was when Timtim and Aku started kissing each other.

"WHAT are you two doing?" yelped Elnor as she jumped off her bed.

"Uhh ohh aah" was about all Timtim could get out as they broke their embrace. Aku started crying again when Timtim abruptly stood up to face Elnor who was now right there by Aku's bed.

"You KNOW that you're not supposed to be doing that unless you've gotten both sets of parents to agree. I'm telling Mr. Jivey when he gets back" barked Elnor as she stomped out the door of the cabin. All the while Sansa and Sukey were just sitting there watching but as Elnor noisily exited, Sansa whispered to Sukey, in a voice we could all pretty much hear, "I'm really starting to dislike Elnor". Sukey remained still and just shook her head but curiously enough she was staring at me the whole time.

I looked around at the others and was surprised to see that Josanna and Wassa were also missing. "Hey, where's WassaJo?" I asked Glukey. He looked at me and his face went white as he looked around the cabin for those two. As if we had a single mind, Glukey and I both got up and walked over to the back door. We hesitated a moment when Sansa called out "Mr. Jivey said not to leave the cabin", but then we stepped out onto the back porch. It was Glukey that saw them first and he nudged me along with whispering "Oh, they're over there and oh boy" and pointing off to the left while smirking.

Evidently, Josanna and Wassa had made up after their little boxing match because they were half-hidden behind a small fir tree about twenty feet away embracing each other. As we both watched, their mouths became glued to each other in that way that you could tell they were much more than just good friends. After a couple seconds of watching them kiss and run their hands all over each other, I figured it was break time and coughed very loudly as both I and Glukey turned sideways so as to not look like we were watching them.

What had attracted our attention, and Glukey's comment, was the intensity between Josanna and Wassa, not the fact that they weren't out there with one of us guys. In our town it wasn't that common but two guys or two girls would occasionally pick each other for marriage instead of a guy and a girl. Heck, Mrs. DeAngelo's last wife died about ten years ago, which also possibly contributed to her being kinda sour-faced in both outlook and appearance since then. Timtim's mother had died when he was about five years old and his father, Mr. Doogra had decided to get married again and this time he married Mr. Hendy. So, like I say, nobody really cared that much about it if two guys or two girls got married, just as long as it was understood that marriage between two people, any two people, lasted until one of them died.

The only time I ever heard of two married people splitting up while they were both alive is the story my father told me, that when he was a kid about a couple where the guy got some sickness in his head and started acting real strangely. Strangely enough that his wife went to the sheriff and mayor at that time and asked what she could do because her husband was doing goofy things like drinking apple cider that had gone sour, chewing on the branches of the apple tree they had out back, and saying words that she couldn't understand at all because they weren't Engrish or any other language we use around here. Well, the mayor and the sheriff went out to talk to the guy and after about an hour or so they agreed with the woman, so the sheriff took the guy out in a boat and they went across the Sealth Sea to someplace where only the sheriff knew about. The sheriff came back about a day and a half later, my dad said, without the guy. When my dad asked his father what happened to the guy, he said his father got quiet and told him that there was an island out there across the sea far to the south where really sick people go and that's where this guy had been taken. Supposedly, out on this island there is, or at least was, a place they called a 'hospital' where they take care of people who go a little funny in the head and can't think well at all anymore. He said it was called McNeil Island but when he told me the story, he said he didn't know if the hospital was still there or not.

But that's the only time I've ever heard of two married people ever being broken apart while both were still living.

In Sultanawash, almost all the older people are married but there are a couple people that make the announcement when they become twenty-one that they are not planning on getting married and would rather live the rest of their life alone. I guess I can understand that because pretty much everyone is friendly to everyone else, so it's not like those single people have to lock themselves away from the rest of us or never have any fun with other people. On the contrary, there are a couple of the singles that say they much prefer not having to worry about anyone other than themselves and I know that there are some married people that tend to frown on that idea, but everyone gets along no matter what their married state is.

What was a bit different with WassaJo was that it was generally understood that younger people, under the age of twenty-one, just didn't carry on with each other the way we were seeing Josanna and Wassa go at it. I had seen Glukey holding hands with Amber, and I had done the same with Sukey and Jellie, but they, and we, never went any further than that. What Josanna and Wassa were now doing was definitely way over the limit in keeping with our customs and traditions.

Sorry, I've been drifting off again from writing about what happened. And really, I need to be very precise on what happened next because it's why I'm where I am right now. Mr. Bacon took pity on me and let me pitch my tent outside the pig-pen jail so I wouldn't suffocate on the odor, but made it very clear that I am still technically 'in jail' while we wait for the trial to begin.

So, there we were, all back on our beds again as Mr. Jivey announced what he had found.

"Nothing at all; I couldn't find Dorman" he rasped out, clearly more frazzled than he had been for a very long time. "I think he may have tried to walk back to town, but who knows. And at this point I don't really give a heck what happened to him. In about ten minutes, we are going to go out and do a remembrance ceremony for Jellie, so take these last few minutes to clear your minds." And with that, he stomped out of the cabin.

* * *

About twenty minutes later, we all gathered once again around the firepit and closed our eyes as Mr. Jivey started the chant again, "Lead us. Guide us. Remember. Lead us. Guide us. Remember." And just as quickly, our minds began filling with images of Jellie. Her smiling face, mischievous grin, that long reddish-blond hair of hers, her laughing at a joke, and my contribution was of that three-legged race and her getting pretty darn familiar with her hands all over me.

Then it happened again.

Jellie was smiling at something someone said to her and that someone then raised their arm and plunged that blade into her chest. Her smile faded as the light in her eyes went out and she fell backward onto the floor as a huge amount of blood poured out around the haft of the knife.

Again, the sheer pain of that act ripped through our minds. My mind finally cleared a few moments later and I found myself on the ground next to the big rock I had previously been sitting on. I looked around and the others were looking pretty mind-fogged, but as a one, they all started staring at me. Glukey looked like he had just swallowed a burning coal while Aku, WassaJo, Timtim, and Sansa had this look of disgust on their faces. Elnor was shaking and turning purple from the effort of holding her emotions inside, while Sukey was just staring at me. Mr. Jivey's face, by contrast, was blank, like his body didn't know what to do.

"My goodness, what the heck happened?" I asked. "Why are you all staring at me?"

Nobody said anything for at least a minute, then Mr. Jivey finally said "Hold out your right hand."

I obediently raised my right arm up and asked "What's the deal? Why do you want to see my hand?" I looked down at my right hand like the others were doing and finally saw what they were looking at.

Many years ago, my parents had given me a piece of their heritage; something that had been done in his family for as long as could be remembered. It wasn't much and it was more a ritual when a son or daughter reached the age of twelve than an actual present. It was a small thin bracelet woven out of some flexible material like nylon but much more durable and sporting an alternating red and yellow spiral design. I remember when they gave it to me and my father fastened it around my wrist, he said "Receive this token of our bloodline and always remember that you are a descendant of people that first inhabited this country ages ago. Be proud of who you are and the great people that went before you, and carry on this tradition with the children that you eventually will have." Then he deftly wove the individual threads this way and that way, then took a piece of smoldering firewood and briefly touched it to the knots he had made. "Now, you will forever wear this as a remembrance of who you are and where you came from. It will never unravel, it will never tear, and you will never be able to remove it; it is a part of you forever just as your ancestors are" he said gravely as he showed a similar bracelet around his right wrist. He then held my right hand tightly with his right hand and leaned forward to touch my forehead with his. After a moment of contact, I could see the memories that he held, the memories that had been passed to him by his father. Old, weatherworn faces looking to the sun high in the sky as they paddled across the sea in large canoes, hundreds of people gathered around a tall thin figure dressed in buckskin adorned with eagle feathers as he led a chant around a newly revealed totem pole, another scene of a younger man tying a similar bracelet around my father's wrist, and so on. Disjointed memories all, but after a few moments I knew where I came from and who I was. It was a ritual that I will never forget and will be sure to pass on to my children, if I ever get to have any. Those, and other memories of my ancestors have occasionally quickly passed through my mind ever since that pairing with my father.

But now, I concentrated and a brief flash of Jellie's last moments went through my mind once more and I knew why they were all staring at me. That hand, the one that held the knife that killed Jellie, had a thin spiral red and yellow bracelet around its wrist, identical to mine.

I had evidently killed Jellie.

Chapter 7 – *Back to Town*

"Wait a minute" I spluttered. "I didn't do it. I DIDN'T DO IT!"

"That's what you say, but we all saw it" barked Elnor. "We saw you stick that knife in Jellie."

That was the signal for them all to start. "Why?", "What the heck did you do that for?", "Poor Jellie and you killed her", and the capper to all the comments "You deserve to be killed yourself".

"But I didn't do it!" I cried one more time. "Why don't you believe me?"

It was Mr. Jivey that answered with "We don't believe you because we all saw it, that's why. Sansa, go in the cabin and get that piece of rope that's by the back door.". Then he stood up and walked over to where I was still half-sprawled on the ground. "Once Sansa gets that rope, we're going to tie your hands up so that you can't harm anyone else."

On cue, Sansa came running back out of the cabin as if her hair was on fire. "Uh…I…Oh…Ahh…" she spluttered as she threw the rope on the ground by Mr. Jivey's feet. "You…come…ooohhhnooo" she blubbered as she more or less crumpled to the ground. Mr. Jivey turned to Timtim and

Glukey and said "You two, stay with EG and make sure he doesn't move" then pivoted and ran back into the cabin.

The next thing we heard was an anguished "OHHHMYGOOOOODDDNNNEEESSSS" and then Mr. Jivey appeared in the cabin doorway looking very ill indeed. The last time I had seen anyone look that bad was when Mr. Jorim tried keeping up with Amboy and had a couple too many swigs from the moonshine bottle and got sooo sick.

All of us, including me, ran over to the cabin, Glukey and Timtim still holding my arms. Mr. Jivey was by now leaning against the front wall of the cabin barfing his guts out on the ground once again. We all looked through the doorway and there was Dorman, or at least what we took to be Dorman. He was lying there on the floor bleeding from it seemed everywhere. There were small cuts on his arms, legs, chest, and a big bruise on his right cheek like someone had whacked him real good with a tree branch or something. There was also a big bloody smash on the top of his head that accounted for the big bloody smear from the back door to where he had been dragged and was now lying. Yes, he was dead.

On seeing that, both Glukey and Timtim grabbed me harder and slammed me against the cabin wall, right next to Mr. Jivey. Elnor immediately came tramping up to stand right next to my face as she screamed "What did you do that for? Why did you kill Dorman? Wasn't it enough that you killed Amber and Jellie that you had to go do it again?" Mr. Jivey turned to look at me, then signaled to Glukey and Timtim to pull my face off the cabin wall. We looked at each other for a moment and then Mr. Jivey roared "You stinking borscht whacker!", then twisted slightly and threw his right fist as hard as he could into my face.

* * *

The next thing I remember is waking up on a stretcher being carried by Glukey and Timtim. I tried to move but found I had been tied down to the stretcher.

"Oh, look. He's awake." Sansa sneered. "We should have just dumped him back a-ways instead of carting him back to town" Elnor added.

"No, we have to take him back so we can perform justice on him" Mr. Jivey replied.

I was about to say something but the whole left side of my face wouldn't work. I could barely move my jaws and couldn't see anything out of my left eye. I figured that my face was pretty swollen from Mr. Jivey's punch, but even so I tried to say something, anything, but all that came out was little blips of noise that didn't make any sense. I was also trying to get over Mr. Jivey calling me a 'borsht-whacker', in other words a completely evil person since only The Devil eats borsht, or olives.

"You just stay quiet and you'll get back to town in one piece" Mr. Jivey threatened as he bent down over my face. "You got a taste of what will happen if you cause any more problems, so don't give me an excuse to hit you again."

"But why are we taking him back?" Sansa asked again. "We should have just tied him up to a tree and let the wolves and whatever else tear him to pieces. Filthy murderer!"

"We agreed after having Dorman's memory service that EG needs to be brought back to town so that justice will be served," said Mr. Jivey.

"But where's the justice of bringing him back when he's killed three people?" asked Glukey. "I still can't believe anyone would hate someone else so much that they would kill them. We should have just left him like Sansa said so that he wouldn't pollute anyone else in town."

I was listening to these comments and getting angrier and angrier by the second. Why were they all so dead-set on me being the guilty one? I didn't do it; *I know* I didn't do it. But where did that memory flash come from? And who would be so evil as to try and make it look like I did it? All these thoughts were going round and round in my brain and I was getting more and more angry; more angry than I think I ever was before in my life. And then I started thinking about what I would do to the real guilty person when I found out who they were. I would punch them, not too hard because I didn't want them to pass out, and then I would hit them again, and again until they told me why they killed Amber, Jellie, and Dorman, and then why they tried to make it look like I did it. And then, I would hit them a couple more times, and throw them in the sea and laugh while they sputtered and tried to stay afloat and …

I stopped myself and thought "What the heck am I doing?". I never got this angry before; even that time when we were playing baseball and Lackey hit that foul ball into my privates. Boy did that hurt, but I didn't get angry about it. Or that time that when Sukey baked that truly horrible tasting apple pie and then smashed a piece of it on top of my head when I told her it wasn't very good. That was embarrassing but I didn't get angry over it. I know Sukey was angry at first but she apologized after doing it and we both laughed it off. What was going on? Everyone seemed so, so *emotional* that it was very strange.

Well, maybe it was because, as far as I knew, nobody had had anything to eat since last night's campfire feast. I know my stomach was growling pretty noisily.

* * *

I must have passed out because the next thing I knew was that my stretcher was laying there on the ground in front of me and I was sitting up against a big old fir tree. I tried moving again but I had been tied to the tree so that I couldn't get up or move a whole lot. My stomach let out a really big growl when I smelled something cooking over a fire about twenty feet away. They were all there sitting around on the ground as Mr. Jivey had something looking like small chickens cooking on a small branch over the fire. It was getting dark so I must have passed out for at least three or four hours. My face was still sore as all get out but at least it appeared to be abating a bit because I was able to manage "I'm really thirsty and I need to go take a pee". At least that's what I thought I said, but nobody seemed to take any interest. So, I tried it again but louder. It hurt like hell but I managed to croak "I need to take a pee" louder, at least I heard it.

Glukey was the nearest to me and evidently, he heard me because he repeated it to the group. To a person, they all turned to stare at me, nothing else, just stares. Mr. Jivey finally got up, told Elnor to keep watch on what was cooking, then came over to me.

“I should let you just pee in your pants but I don’t think anyone wants to keep smelling that until we get back to town. Timtim, come over here and help me untie him.”

Timtim obligingly walked over and helped Mr. Jivey untie the knots located on the other side of the tree from where I was sitting. Mr. Jivey then said “The two of us are going to walk you out a little bit and then you can go pee, but don’t try anything or I’ll hit you again, except harder this time, you little olive-sucker.”

I didn’t think much of it then, but Mr. Jivey was really getting on my nerves; first calling me a borsht-whacker and now an olive-sucker. I mean, he just called me about the worst things that could ever be said about a person since borsht and olives are two of the most evil things there are.

The three of us stumbled a bit but managed to get out about twenty or thirty yards from the makeshift camp. Mr. Jivey then said “Ok, go pee”.

“You want me to go pee with you watching? I don’t know if I can do that” I kinda sorta mumbled. My jaw seemed to be loosening up a bit but it was still pretty much a stretch to actually speak.

“We’re not letting you out of our sight, so you gotta pee, you go pee right here right now, or we just march you back to the tree and tie you up again” snarled Mr. Jivey. I couldn’t remember ever hearing him talk in that tone before. Timtim meanwhile just stood there with this look of something, maybe hatred, on his face. He picked up a small branch and started whacking some of the ferns and shrubs that were there, then abruptly grabbed both ends in his hands and broke the branch in two as he snapped out "You don't deserve anything, not for what you did. I think we should just snap you in two like this branch here. It's people like you that give the rest of us a bad reputation."

I was getting pretty afraid of those two and what might happen if I delayed any longer, so I hesitantly unzipped and let loose on a small molehill. Relief coursed through me and I could actually feel the tension lessening throughout my body. Finally, I finished, zipped up, and turned to both of them. "I didn't do it. I don't know how that memory was ever made but it wasn't me. Someone must have figured out how to make a bracelet like mine, because I wasn't anywhere near Jellie back then. I was with you right before Jellie was found, don't you remember?" I asked of Mr. Jivey.

"That's neither here nor there, we all saw it" Mr. Jivey replied, but with this sudden far-off look in his eyes like he was trying to remember what really happened. "Enough! Back to the campfire, both of you" he said as he still stood there motionless. Abruptly he must have come to some decision because he quit looking up into the trees and stared at us, then made shooing motions towards us.

About twenty minutes later, Sukey walked over and gave me a small piece of whatever they had cooked over the fire; I think it was quail but can't be sure. I had been tied to the tree again after I was allowed to pee, so Sukey held the little piece to my mouth so I could grab it with my teeth and eat it.

"I could just shove this down your throat so you choke on it and die" she growled in a low tone, "but Mr. Jivey says you have to have something to eat, otherwise you won't make it back to town."

I tried replying but it wasn't easy with my sore face and full mouth by saying yet one more time "I didn't do it" but it came out more like "I diwant dute".

"I don't care what you say, we all saw it."

I managed to swallow, which was a bit difficult because Sukey hadn't brought anything to drink to wash it down with, and then said "I don't know how that person did it, but I didn't".

Sukey got this odd look on her face as she said "You're such a pig, look at you. You got little shreds all over your mouth and chin." And then Sukey did something that I wasn't expecting and was totally out-of-character for her. Her eyes almost melted into something I don't know what as she bent down and licked my lips and chin, then planted the wettest, juiciest kiss full on my lips. I was caught completely off-guard and didn't respond in the least, at least not until her tongue slid in between my lips and curled around my tongue. At that point, I tried pulling my head back but she quickly reached both her hands around the back of my head and pulled me into her face, keeping the by-now ferocious lip-lock she had on me. I started squirming and trying to break her hold until she finally broke off after another couple seconds.

"What *is* your problem?" she snapped quietly between gasps as she pulled back a couple inches. "You should be thrilled that I like you enough to kiss you. Maybe I'll get a chance to come back in an hour or two when the rest of them are asleep, but you'll just have to wait. Hmm, I think I like that idea, *a lot*."

I was completely dumbfounded by her behavior and her words so I just sat there like a bump on a log. After another second or two, she just said "Hmmph", got back up, and walked back to where the others were by now setting up fir branches and blankets to sleep on. Halfway there she turned back to me and smiled, an evil smile as if she was hungry or something, but like I had never seen before in my life; part mischievous and part something else but what that something else was I had no idea.

I really didn't have the foggiest idea what had just happened, what I should have done, or what was happening to all of us. But I do know that I had this fire burning inside me now, something I'd never felt before in my whole life. I also know that if I hadn't been tied to that god-forsaken tree, I would have done anything, absolutely *anything*, if Sukey had asked me to do it.

I was brought out of my thoughts when I heard Mr. Jivey call out "WassaJo? Where are you two?"

"Oh noooo! Not again!!" wailed Aku as she broke into tears again.

Just then, both Wassa and Josanna came stumbling out of the scantly lit scrub trees, both mumbling something about having to go pee, then sat down by the fire.

I noticed that nobody else seemed to pay attention to the fact that Josanna and Wassa both appeared to be wearing each other's sweaters, like while they had gone off into the woods, they had exchanged clothes. Another thing that tickled my brain a bit, but I didn't really pay further attention to it.

The only thing on my mind at that point was "What's going to happen to me?".

Chapter 8 - *The Deputy Prosecutor of Washida Steps In*

My name is Geena Lambskin and I work for the greater territory of Washida in the law and justice department. I'm going to interrupt the written records of Eaglefeeder Whitehorse at this point and insert some background information on this case that I've found out to date because it's the rule in our department to write down everything that happens right after it happens, so that an accurate recording of all pertinent information is available in case anyone wants to go back afterward and contest the outcome. The trial of Eaglefeeder is set to begin in four days so I'm going to compile what information I have so I can make an attempt at finding the truth of what happened at the Wilderness Cabin when we do start the trial. But first, I have to clarify some history in order to put this whole affair, as well as my part of the story, in proper perspective, and also have to restate the basic principles that I, in my capacity as Deputy Prosecutor, have to follow in order to make the final determination in this or any other case that comes before our department.

I was taught that a long time ago, many generations ago, the world was very different. Villages, towns, and cities were spread all over the world and in order to keep order amongst the citizens of these places, governments were created.

These governments were composed of people either elected by the people or appointed by other electees. Parts of these governments were charged with what was then termed 'law and order', in other words, some rules of conduct were put in place, these were called 'the laws', while some people were appointed to make sure that people followed the laws, and this is where the term order comes into the picture. There is a third leg of society that people often confuse with the term 'law' and that is 'justice'.

In my mind, and as written in the law of the land, society creates laws that are meant to govern the actions of the people for the purpose of keeping the peace or 'order' so to speak. People in general are fairly well-mannered, but when one or a few of those people decide that they are going to enforce their own will upon the others, either through violent or other criminal acts, the laws are set to deter those actions. The majority of society will recognize that these behaviors and acts are repugnant and not to be condoned, so the laws forbid those behaviors and provide for a means of deterring those individuals from committing those acts through forms of punishment that escalate in magnitude in relation to the law being broken.

However, 'justice' is a concept that provides for either an elevation or a mitigation of the punishment according to the situation and circumstances of the broken law. Therefore, if a person is the subject of a criminal act, but they themselves commit a further criminal act to deter the first act, for instance if person one has a cow and person two tries to steal that cow and person one repeatedly punches person two to stop the theft, then justice comes into play and says person one should be forgiven for breaking the law which says violence towards another is a crime, but person two will still be liable for breaking the law in attempting to steal another person's property. This is the concept of 'justice' and it is a partner to both 'law' and 'order'. All three components are necessary to keep society relatively healthy, relatively well-mannered, and respectful of each other and their differing ways of life.

So that is where I come into this picture. I work in the Department of Law and Justice along with Mr. Spencer, Mrs. Alotto, and Mrs. Densmore and we're responsible for resolving disputes in this territory. Our building is located in downtown Wenatchawash so we're closer to the people out on the west end of the territory, and to tell the truth, we haven't heard much from the eastern side of the territory. There is another office out in Spokawash but like I said, we haven't heard from them in at least months. Lord knows, most of the time we don't have much at all to do but every now and then someone out there acts up a bit too much and we have to come and figure out the situation. About four months ago, I had to go to Skykowash to settle a complaint between two families that each claimed a section of the riverbank there. Actually, it wasn't that big of a deal because the ultimate resolution was that the area in question just had to be divided into two sections. When I interviewed both parties involved, I found that the grandfather of one of the families had very large feet and when he paced out his section, the size of his boots meant that the people owning the section next to his got shorted a bit. It wasn't that difficult to figure out but it kept me busy for a couple days. Otherwise, I don't really have that much to do since the other three deputies take most of the other more involved jobs like that one case where a vagrant, some people call them 'stump-jumpers', actually punched a person in the town of Yakiwash. That was a big deal and took Mr. Spencer a whole week and a half to settle.

I am digressing a bit from this particular narrative so let me get back to the facts in this case.

A Mr. Jorim from Sultanawash came riding into town three days ago and when he finally found our office, I was the only one there so he explained the situation to me. At first, I was feeling pretty happy about taking on the case but as I listened to what he had to say, I became more and more horrified by what I heard. I had never even heard about a person killing another person and it just struck me as completely evil and despicable. Why would a person do that? I resolved to take the case and go back with Mr. Jorim to Sultanawash to bring the culprit to justice. I've now spent the last two days searching through the old files for something similar so that I can perhaps be able to reach a morally easier conclusion but I really haven't found much of any help. About the closest I was able to come is the case of Mr. Ninivu's dog that was killed because it attacked Mr. Gates' chickens. And that was about all I've been able to find. I'll just have to trust my instincts and the law as written to guide me in determining what to do about this Eaglefeeder Whitehorse.

This will be one of only a couple times that I've had to journey so far; two long days on horseback to get from Wenatchawash to Sultanawash. Mr. Jorim at first tried to get me to talk to him out of politeness I guess, but I spent a good part of each day on my horse in research using my

Micoazonon helmet; asking this and that question to see what the archives had. We deputies have a special section in Micoazonon where we store all our files so I was able to go back through at least a hundred years'-worth of cases and notes by other deputies. As I stated before, I could not find one single instance of one person killing another person. I might have to see if I can get access to the locked files from previous time periods for any similar cases, but as that requires a unanimous vote of all current deputies and since we haven't had word from Mrs. Alotto in the last three weeks ever since she rode over to the Spokawash office, it's very doubtful that I'll get access. And I do feel a bit sorry for Mr. Jorim and his attempts to engage me in conversation; he does seem like a nice guy but I'm sorry, business first.

It has been a pleasant ride for me; I don't get a chance to ride very often for such a distance. Mostly, I spend my days tending to my garden where I grow a variety of vegetables and berries including blueberries, raspberries, squash, tomatoes, and green beans. One year I tried growing peapods but they became so full that they actually took over and my green beans suffered as a result. I do enjoy doing a quick steaming of green beans and quartered tomatoes, so I haven't grown any peapods for the last couple years. Besides, my neighbor, Mrs. Toyosan, really likes peapods and consequently grows a lot of them, so we swap beans for peapods every year. She quick-cooks the pea pods along with corn, mushrooms, and onions and then mixes them in with fried thin noodles she makes out of wheat flour. She said her mother used to talk about when they used something called 'rice', evidently some kind of grass seed, instead of the noodles, but attempts to grow rice out here always failed, so she just uses the noodles. Mrs. Toyosan said that one time her mother tried to cook some of the other various grass seeds as a substitute for the rice but that didn't work out well at all.

But, all in all, I have a pleasant life where I really don't have to work all that often. I'm free to grow my garden and spend time doing research through the data archives. I like reading all about the cases my office has worked through the years because it gives me a background in how people's lives have changed. For instance, back a generation or two, those Micoazanon drones were less frequent than they are now. Now, a day doesn't pass when at least one of them zooms over Wenatchawash, and seeing them flying along, tying all the various towns together into one big spiderweb of humanity, just seems to put one in a better, more happy mood.

* * *

It was a funny yet strange breakthrough in thinking that I just had. We're within an hour or two of getting to Sultanawash and it hit me; I'm wearing the Micoazanon helmet to do all this research yet Micoazanon connects everyone to their main site through a system, so why can't I connect to someone else that is using Micoazanon? The helmet listens to what we say and can read some of our thoughts, so maybe if I concentrate on reaching the other deputies, I can explain to them the situation I'm in and make that request to get into the locked files? As soon as we get to Sultanawash and I get some place to set up and work, I'm going to try it. I'm thinking that maybe there's a way if I can't actually reach a person, maybe I can leave them a written note or maybe even the sound of my voice as a message? I'll have to do some more research on that because there just has to be a way to do it. I mean, there were a whole lot more people in the world a long time ago before the floods and they had to be able to talk to each other even if they were located miles apart, didn't they?

***

It worked! I was able to get through to Mr. Spencer, Mrs. Alotto, and Mrs. Densmore as they were on their own cases and I got them to approve my access to the locked files. I'm going to just wait a while before attempting that because I'm just not sure what to look for at this time. Maybe when I interview the people involved in this case, I'll have a better idea of just what I might need to look for. Who knows, I might not even need to get into those files? I just wonder why using the helmet hasn't been thought of before for communicating with other people; I mean it's just a great thing to be able to talk to someone that can be miles away though I do suppose one could get addicted pretty easily to this near-instantaneous method of communicating with distant people. I can just see Mrs. Densmore wearing her helmet all the time because she is just so chatty a person that I know she'd like to be able to talk to anyone and everyone that she knows.

Anyway, I think I have what I need to at least start investigating this case but I'm sure when I really get into it, I'll need to do some deep thinking to clear this whole matter up.

Chapter 9 - *My Trial Begins*

I've been waiting for so long that the old pigsty jail I pitched my tent against doesn't really smell that much anymore. I guess it's been about eight days since we got back to town. It took the better part of two days-worth of hiking to get back here. After that first night on the trail back, we had a quick breakfast of some berries and then Mr. Jivey took pity on Glukey and Timtim, especially since we had an unseasonal little drizzle that started up for about a quarter of an hour, and made me walk with the others except my hands were tied in front of me. I remember as I was munching away on those berries, memories of Sukey's actions from the night before flitted through my head, but as Elnor was the one who gave me the berries I didn't get a chance to ask Sukey just what had been going through her mind when she kissed me. That memory still haunts me since I don't have anything else I can do while officially 'under arrest' as Mr. Bacon put it. I really don't understand what that means since the only thing I can see that I'm under is my tent. I'm still a bit sore in places where I guess I got punched or kicked, but most of the bruises are now pretty much gone. It was a good idea that Mrs. Lambskin told me to write down everything I remembered because, to tell the truth, for about two or three days after we got back from camp it was still a bit difficult to really talk that much.

So, about three days ago, I started writing everything down in the notebook that Mrs. Lambskin gave me. She's a bit screwy sort of person; all serious like for most of the time, but now and then she'll say something like "corpis delectal" and "sub-penising" which doesn't mean anything to me, but then she'll smirk and tell me "Just the facts, write down just the facts". What does she think I'll do? Write down something that didn't happen?

Anyway, I understand she's gone around to the other people that were on the trip, starting with Mr. Jivey, and taken down notes of what they've told her happened out there. She even went so far as to have Mr. Jivey take her out to the campsite and walk her through what happened where, as if she couldn't understand what he told her without having to actually see it also.

Mr. Bacon wanted to go out there so he could take care of Amber, Jellie, and Dorman's bodies, but Mrs. Lambskin told him no since as the sheriff he had to watch me so that I didn't run away. So, Mr. Jubal and Mr. Adanto hitched up the horses to one of the wagons and set out along with Mrs. DeAngelo, Mrs. Lambskin, and Mr. Jivey to go retrieve Amber, Jellie, and Dorman's bodies. They left early one morning and got back around sunset the same day. After getting back, Mrs. DeAngelo came to see me and started getting on me about having to burn in hell for doing what I did. Luckily, Mrs. Lambskin was near and heard her and stopped her by saying that she didn't want to 'prejuice the case', whatever that meant.

That next day, there was a town remembrance ceremony where just about everyone showed up, all one thousand two hundred and forty people. Most everyone knows most everyone else so they were all interested in what happened. This is the first time in a long time that everyone showed up for the ceremony; the last time this happened was years ago when that hunting party tried climbing Glacier Peak to round up some mountain goats and there was a landslide and four of them got trapped and died. But I was a little kid at that time and can't remember much of the details. Of course, I wasn't invited or permitted to attend the remembrance ceremony for Amber, Jellie, and Dorman because Mrs. DeAngelo said I would 'poison the ceremony with my evil thoughts'. Even so, after the ceremony was over, Mr. Bacon came by to check on me and said that it wasn't as comfortable or joyous as those ceremonies usually are. He said there were some dark thoughts that happened but wouldn't say just what they were. Mrs. Lambskin did participate in the ceremony so as to gain background information on Amber, Jellie, and Dorman so she could better figure out just what happened.

Even so, the day after the ceremony, five days after we got back from camp and on the afternoon of Mrs. Lambskin's arrival, I was feeling a lot better about things. Even the thoughts about Sukey kinda faded away.

When we first got back there was a bit of a stir because we were back so early so Mr. Jivey related what had happened to Mr. Joniak because, as the mayor, he needed to know, and Mr. Bacon because as sheriff, he was expected to know what to do with me until everything got resolved. Well, Mrs. DeAngelo also got into it as Mr. Joniak's advisor and I guess she went off on a rant about 'burning in hell' and such and

Mr. Bacon figured he'd better get me put away somewhere just to keep Mrs. DeAngelo from maybe burning my parent's house down if I was left to stay there until things got sorted out. When Mrs. Lambskin got here, Mr. Jivey had to retell his story to her. Mrs. DeAngelo wanted a trial set up as soon as Mrs. Lambskin got here but Mrs. Lambskin said that this was a very difficult case and she had to have enough time to figure it out, so my trial was postponed for ten days. So, it'll start the day after tomorrow.

Mrs. Lambskin is an interesting person. When I first related my story, and then gave her this journal to read, she spent a lot of time just sitting there; I guess absorbing all what I told her. Every now and then she'd put on the Micoazanon helmet, walk out the door and I'd then hear her saying something to the helmet; I guess she was dictating notes to herself about my case. In any event, I'm not really that worried about what I told her but I am worried about those memories that got shared where it appears I actually did do it. I'll write it down again; I didn't kill anyone, but… I have no explanation for those memories showing that I did.

* * *

Well, from now on this narrative is going to be a combination of Eaglefeeder's memories and my investigation since that's the only way I think it will make sense for the records. I've interviewed most everyone involved with this situation and am still confused a bit about what really happened. According to Mr. Jivey, the only person with the red and yellow bracelet that was seen in the group remembrance ceremony is Eaglefeeder Whitehorse. That would seem to put an end to this whole matter, but yet, just before the second victim, Jellie Overholser, was found, Eaglefeeder and Mr. Jivey were together in a conversation about what happened to the first victim, Amber Ducommon. That casts a shadow of doubt over whether Eaglefeeder really did kill Jellie, and by extension, the other two as well. And then there's the unsettling memory fragments that came up during that group remembrance ceremony, which one might expect if Eaglefeeder was there since he's the one accused of killing those other kids. But he wasn't permitted to attend, so just where, or rather from whom did those memories come from?

So, there's doubt there whether Eaglefeeder is the culprit responsible for these horrid crimes. And then also, I can't entirely discount the thought that perhaps there are two, or possibly more than two people that have committed these crimes. But that idea is so far down the list of possibilities that I really don't want to go there just now.

There is good news in this investigation though; I've gotten approval to go into the Micoazanon archive files to do some research. I've just got to figure this one out but even when I do, what am I supposed or expected to do about it? That's where those archives will help and guide me.

* * *

Mr. Joniak, the mayor, just came by a bit ago and told me that tomorrow morning, everyone involved is expected to be at the town center for my trial to begin. He hopes that there is enough room in the center hall but I told him that since we regularly have town parties there with a couple hundred people, there should be enough room. He just shrugged his shoulders and said this is a once in a lifetime event and so most of the townsfolk might show up. He wasn't very nice about it and said some other things that made me think that he's going to have to order Mr. Bacon to take me over to McNeil Island. I don't want to go there. My parents have come by every day to visit me and I sure don't want to have them live the rest of their lives with the memory of me being cast out. I'm scared of what's going to happen.

* * *

Oh, my goodness! I can't believe what I've found in the locked archives. According to the histories, people used to kill other people for no other reason than they just had a disagreement. I can't seem to be able to believe that; it's just so…so horrible to imagine. People would meet on a street in their town and because one claimed 'a parking space', whatever that is, as their own and another person thought they had claim to it, sometimes there would be a fight that sometimes would escalate into one of them killing the other. My hands are shaking as I write this down because it is such a completely abhorrent and atrociously *evil* act that I can barely imagine it happening. Were our ancestors so self-centered that they didn't consider any other human life to be worth saving at all costs, that they in of themselves were so important that nothing and nobody else mattered? My stomach is literally rolling over and I don't know if I can keep from being violently ill after reading those files. My hands are shaking too much and I need to go take a walk and see if I can harden myself to doing further research.

* * *

I've calmed down a bit from reading those ancient files and set the beginning of the trial for ten o'clock this morning. I've told Mr. Joniak that he will be the person responsible for keeping order during the trial since, as the mayor, everyone should already be used to following what he says and therefore there won't be any problems. He, in return, told me he really doesn't know what else he can do other than keeping people quiet which really is all I want him to do. I, as the deputy prosecutor, am supposed to go over the facts of the case, ask each involved person what they saw, and then tie up and present the conclusions that necessarily follow. It is then up to Mr. Joniak to ask the townspeople gathered if they believe what I say or not.

I've gone through all the statements from the witnesses and, added to my own observations, I've put together a story of what might have happened out there at the Wilderness Camp.

But… I do have a problem with what I've put together. On the face of everything, it looks like Eaglefeeder Whitehorse did kill those three other youths. There are the memories from the attendees at the memorial ceremonies that clearly show he did kill Jellie Overholser. But… that conclusion is reached solely because of that bracelet he has on his wrist, and who is to say that someone else didn't copy that bracelet and use it to implicate Eaglefeeder? Another nagging thought that keeps coming back is that just prior to when Jellie's body was found, Eaglefeeder and Mr. Jivey had been discussing at some length what had happened to the first victim, Amber Ducommon, which means that the time window for Eaglefeeder to kill Jellie was almost nonexistent. But on the other hand, I have interviewed everyone that was out there at the camp and cannot think of any one of them that had a reason, or the opportunity, to kill those three people. Even Eaglefeeder, after talking to him repeatedly at great length, doesn't seem to have any reason to have done it either.

So, am I back to square one with this matter? Nobody had a motive for the crimes, no single person had the opportunity, and yet, there are three dead people that deserve to have their killer brought to justice.

Well, we'll see what comes out of the trial. I need to clear my mind and present what knowledge I've amassed. I'll have to set my Micoazanon helmet to record so that I can later transcribe everything that is said at the trial for my personal files, but whatever the helmet records will still be the official record of the trial.

* * *

Official transcript follows:

Mrs. Lambskin, Deputy Prosecutor for the territory of Washida: *"For the record, this proceeding is the trial of Eaglefeeder Whitehorse in the matter of the illegal deaths of Amber Ducommon, Jellie Overholser, and Dorman DiFazio, being held in the town of Sultanawash, territory of Washida, on this date, September 9th of the year 1637 of the post-flood era. Mr. Mayor, you can now speak."*

Mr. Joniak, the Mayor of Sultanawash: *"People, quiet down, quiet down. We are here to listen to the Deputy Prosecutor's explanation of the facts concerning the* *illegal deaths of Amber, Jellie, and Dorman. Please stay calm and just listen to what Mrs. Lambskin says. We need to hear everything she says before we can figure out what really happened out there at the Wilderness Camp. Mrs. Lambskin will talk and then there will be an opportunity for anyone and everyone to ask questions, but let her talk first."*

[murmuring]

Mr. Joniak, the Mayor of Sultanawash: *"People, I said quiet down. A chance for anyone and everyone to say or ask anything will come later. Mrs. Lambskin, please begin."*

Mrs. Lambskin, Deputy Prosecutor for the territory of Washida: *"Good people of the town of Sultanawash, I am here to relate the story of what happened at the Wilderness Camp. I have compiled what I am about to tell you from talking to all those people involved including all those that were out at the camp as well as other people from Sultanawash that know or knew both the dead people or the accused, Eaglefeeder Whitehorse. I believe it is a true retelling of what happened but there are still some questions I have ..."*

Person identified as Raindrum Whitehorse: *"Of course he didn't do it. I did it; I confess, I killed those three people."*

[loud shouting from multiple people]

Mrs. Lambskin, Deputy Prosecutor for the territory of Washida: *"WHAT? THAT CAN'T BE! You couldn't* *have done it; you're trying to protect your son – I KNOW you didn't do it!"*

[loud shouting from multiple people]

Mr. Joniak, the Mayor of Sultanawash: *"People! QUIET DOWN!" "Mrs. Lambskin, I think you need to go back and do some more research." "People, in light of what Mr. Whitehorse just said, I think we need to adjourn this proceeding; COURT IS ADJOURNED."*

Chapter 10 – *What a Mess to Unravel!*

I'm certainly glad that the helmet automatically stopped recording when Mr. Joniak roared "court is adjourned", otherwise it would have caught my "HOLY CANOLA!" remark. I have to watch that because the rest of the deputies will probably give me a month or two off from my job if they hear me swear like that. I don't normally swear, well, at least not *that* much, let alone invoke Canola, oil of the gods, but I just couldn't help myself. Thankfully, I don't think anyone really paid that much attention to me after Mr. Whitehorse said that he had done the murders. The only way I can describe the scene afterward is 'pandemonium', although I've never really been witness to something like that before, but I've heard from the other deputies that that used to happen sometimes when big crowds used to assemble in the old days.

However, even though Mr. Whitehorse confessed to the murders, I don't believe him for a second. I think he is just trying to take the blame so that his son doesn't get taken away to McNeil Island. Which, of course, doesn't make any sense because neither will ever see each other no matter if he or his son get taken away.

My problem has now increased dramatically; I mean, how can I possibly present any retelling of what happened and have the townspeople approve my story? If I present the story and it turns out Eaglefeeder is the person most likely to have committed those murders, there will undoubtably still be some of the townspeople that will take his father's confession to heart and not believe a word I say. And the details of the happening just really don't support Mr. Whitehorse being the culprit no matter how I twist and turn them.

What am I going to do? About the only thing I can think of right now is finding some place quiet and out of the way and doing more research with the Micoazanon helmet. Maybe I can use it to contact the other deputies and see what they think.

Why did I jump at taking this case?

* * *

I can't believe my Dada actually confessed to killing Amber, Jellie, and Dorman. I *know* he didn't do it; he couldn't have. He is the most kind, gentle father a kid could ask for. He never raises his voice and whenever anything comes up that he disagrees with, or doesn't turn out quite right, like that lamb stew he made that one time that really wasn't very edible at all, he just sits back and says something like "well, that didn't turn out so good so it's one more thing I've learned". I didn't get a chance to talk to him at all because as soon as Mr. Joniak adjourned the trial, Mr. Bacon took him away after telling me I was now free again and could return home. My mother hasn't stopped crying since Dada was taken away and I think she'll probably try to talk Mr. Bacon into letting her talk to Dada, so I'm pretty much alone again.

But I do have to say our house sure smells a lot better than the jail.

I know I didn't kill the others and I really can't believe Dada did it either, so now what? Mrs. Lambskin looked all out of sorts and is holed up again in the room she's renting from Mrs. Herula, doing what I haven't a clue. I guess if anyone is going to figure this out, sad to say, I don't think it will be Mrs. Lambskin, so I'd better look over my notes again and go talk to the others that were out there at camp and see maybe I can put this together and figure it out.

I was able to find Timtim right after the trial broke up and people were still crowded outside the center all discussing what Dada had said.

"Hey, Timtim. I need to talk to you" I said as I grabbed him by the arm and steered him around the back of the center. "Do you honestly think I did it?"

He looked at me pretty hard for a second or two and then said "I really don't know, I mean I don't think you did and I sure as heck hope you didn't, but I just don't know for sure", then turned away and started walking.

I grabbed his arm again and spun him around, then said "I just want to tell you I didn't do it. I know that sounds like exactly what I should be saying if I did it, but I didn't do it; I promise I didn't do it. C'mon now, we've been friends all our lives; do you think I'm capable of doing something like that?"

He stared at me again for another couple seconds, then said "Honestly, I don't think so but there was that memory of you holding the knife and …"

"You know as well as I do that someone else could have faked that and then fed that memory into the ceremony. Think about what you saw – that hand with the bracelet, was it suntanned like mine or more whitish? Was it a big hand like mine or a small hand? Think back and then tell me what you saw."

"You know, that Mrs. Lambskin never asked me for those specific details. Hmm, let me go back to my house where it's quiet" – he swept his hand to indicate the small groups of people still milling about – "and I'll see if I can remember anything. Now, just let me be by myself for a bit."

I looked around for a bit more until I finally spotted Glukey, Sukey, and Lackey standing there talking to each other and walked up to them.

"Hey Sukey" I said. "Do you really think I did it? What about you" I said as I turned to Glukey. "We've been friends for how long, I mean we've known each other for so many years. Do you think I did it?"

Sukey just glared at me for an instant and then cut off Glukey who had just opened his mouth to say something with "I don't know what to think of you. We've known you for a long time but I'm not sure about anything anymore. I mean, c'mon now, your father said he did it, so what are we to believe? If he's capable of doing it, doesn't that mean that you as his son is also capable of it?" Sukey always seemed to have it in for me, always watching my every move and making a comment.

"Yeah" said Glukey, "I just don't know what to believe anymore. We were such good friends and I just can't believe that you would have taken Amber from me, especially like that. I just don't know anything anymore I guess."

Lackey was just standing there listening to the other two talk and when Glukey finished, she just said "Well, I wasn't there so I don't know what went on but I can't believe you would have done anything like that. You were always fun-loving and fun to be around, even though you did kinda ignore Sukey when she got that crush on you" she said as she got a mischievous little look on her face as she turned to Sukey.

Sukey's face got flaming red and immediately she came back with "I do *not* have a crush on EG" and stomped off towards their house.

I looked at Lackey and asked "Does she really like me that much?"

"She used to mention you every now and then, you know, and that always made me think that she was sweet on you" was Lackey's comment back to me.

Glukey just looked at Lackey and said "Nooo, she doesn't, I mean she didn't like you *that* much, at least I didn't think she did" while looking a bit puzzled.

"Well, remember how she'd ask if you were going to see EG or if he was coming by our place? You never saw the light that came into her eyes when she heard EG was coming by." And with that, Lackey turned and headed back to their place.

"Girls. I guess I'll never understand them" was the only thing Glukey said before turning aside and following Lackey.

"Hmm" I said to myself. "I never knew Sukey was that fond of me. I wonder…" but then cut that thought off at the pass as I looked for Mr. Jivey in the slowly departing crowd.

I finally spotted him moseying his way towards his little house a block away from the town center and quickened my steps until I caught up with him.

"Mr. Jivey? Can I talk to you?" I asked.

He stopped and turned towards me then said "I don't know what I can talk to you about; I mean Mrs. Lambskin told me not to talk to anyone about what I saw or heard back at the camp."

"I really don't want to talk about that; I just wanted to know if you thought I did it." And as his face clouded over, I changed that to "I mean, do you think I'm capable of doing that?"

"I thought I knew you before we went out to the camp but I'm not just sure anymore. I mean, I thought I knew every one of you kids before we went out there but then with that fight that happened and the name calling, I'm not sure of a whole lot anymore." He paused and swallowed once or twice and then said "If it's any consolation to you, no, I don't think you did it. But..." and that puzzled look came over his face again, "...there was that memory of your bracelet. I just can't get over that vision we all saw."

"You think it's possible someone else out there has a bracelet like mine? I mean, my father says that it's a tradition passed down in our family, so who's to say that I don't have some relative out there with the same bracelet?"

"Now, that's a thought I never had before. I wonder..." and he turned and resumed rambling off to his house, all the while with that same confused look on his face that meant he was really thinking hard about something. I had seen that look more than a couple times during school when someone would ask him a difficult question that wasn't quite answered in the school books, like the time Sukey asked just what 'patriotism' was. I remember he had a hard time explaining how it was like loyalty to your family or friends, but bigger than that, like to your whole town or collection of towns in your region. I think we all got the picture after he got through but Mr. Jivey was sweating at the end of his explanation, always a good indication that he was putting a lot of thought and effort into answering the question.

I turned to walk back to our house when I saw Mama hurrying down towards the jail. I was able to stop her but she tried to push past me while saying "Let me go, I have to see your father". I stood my ground and asked her point blank "You don't think Dada did it, do you? Any more than me being able to do it?"

She just shook her head and replied "I *know* your father didn't do it because he was here with me the whole-time you kids were gone, and I can't believe you would do such a thing. Now, let me go so I can talk to Mr. Bacon and Mr. Joniak" and she broke off and resumed trotting towards the jail.

"If Dada was here all the time, he couldn't have done it, and I'm pretty sure I didn't do it, so who did?" I asked myself. "I need to go talk to Mrs. Lambskin about that vision."

* * *

"What a mess, what a big nuking mess" I kept repeating to myself as I walked back to my room at Mrs. Herula's house. I had put the story together of what I thought happened and yes, there were some holes in it, but overall, it seemed to show that Eaglefeeder did the murders. What capped it all off was that vision that everyone had in the sharing experience.

"Wait" I said out loud as it suddenly hit me. All along I, along with everyone else, has accepted that vision as the absolute truth, but what if it could be faked?

"Crappeeshla," I said, using yet another swear word that could get me suspended, "I need to review everyone's stories *without* their recollections of that vision. I need to know where everyone was when those murders happened. I need to throw out my original story and start all over again. I need to find out if memories can be faked. I need to talk to Eaglefeeder."

Chapter 11 – *A Path We Shouldn't Have Taken*

Instead of walking back to my house, I turned down Rainier Avenue to go to Mrs. Herula's. I was going to try and talk to Mrs. Lambskin about that vision from Jellie's remembrance session. I know I didn't do it but that darned, excuse my franko, vision we all had is going to cook my goose if I, or she and I, can't figure out what really happened. What is really odd about that vision is I swear it didn't come from me; I would have remembered it and actually felt that memory if it came from me, but when I saw it as it passed through my mind, I didn't feel anything. That's the funny thing about those shared memories; you actually feel your own memory as you share it and since I didn't feel it, it could not have been mine. Either that or I really am the cold-blooded murderer that people think I am. I really need to talk to Mrs. Lambskin about that. She'll realize that since I didn't feel anything, other than the horror of sticking a knife in someone else, it could not have been a memory that came from me. We'll have to work together to figure out just who was where when it all happened and that will certainly show that at the very least, I could not have done it.

* * *

Ok, so let's assume that that memory vision was somehow faked, now where do I start? I need to talk to Eaglefeeder about maybe there is some other person in his family with that bracelet, someone other than his father. Maybe his father has some relatives that don't live around here but maybe live out by the Wilderness Camp? But then, even if there are some cousins or uncles or something out there, why would they pick this specific time to be killing someone at the camp? Oh my, I just thought of something – maybe there's some spirit of his ancestors out there roaming around? No, but that doesn't make any sense since spirits and ghosts don't really exist; when a person dies, they die and that's the last of them. But maybe here's another thought. My mind is just racing now. What if the spirit of one of those ancestors manifested itself in EG's mind? His father, Raindrum Whitehorse, told me about the bracelet as a symbol of all of their ancestors and how they shared memories when EG was only twelve, so maybe there's something there?

Whoa, what am I doing? I've got all these ideas buzzing in my mind and I must be getting a little goofy, I mean thinking about ghosts and long-dead spirits taking over a person's mind? No no, there's got to be a rational explanation for all this. The shared memories show that it was a real person that killed these kids, not some ghosts. I need to calm down some and sit down with EG and figure this out.

* * *

"Can I come in?" I asked Mrs. Lambskin after I knocked on Mrs. Herula's door.

"I was just thinking I needed to talk to you to get this all straightened out. First off, let me see that bracelet you wear."

I thrust out my right arm and pulled back my shirtsleeve. "See, it's just a simple thing that my father gave me when I was twelve as a way of connecting to my ancestors. He put it on and then poked it with a piece of firewood that was on fire and told me it'll never come off."

Mrs. Lambskin held my hand and twisted my wrist this way and that as she looked at it, then finally grabbed it with her thumb and forefinger and tugged at it.

"See, I told you it won't come off."

"Hmm, this is an interesting piece of work. I don't think I've ever seen anything like it before" she said as she continued eyeing it. "It is pretty nice I have to admit. Oh, hey, here's a thought. The Micoazanon helmet has a built-in scanner so I wonder what it'll say if I scan it. Here, hold your arm out while I grab the helmet." She grabbed her helmet off the table and held it next to my arm as she said to the helmet "What is this?".

There was a moment or two of little lights sparkling on the helmet and then it said in a flat monotone "Item is a wrist bracelet of unknown manufacture. Analysis, database search, and comparison of x-ray crystallography indicate presence of titanium, silver, manganese, simple carbon compounds, and several plastic compounds including polyacrylate, phenol-formaldehyde, paradichlorohexane, with trace amounts of …"

“That’s enough” she said to cut it off from reciting more stuff neither of us understood. “What I wanted to know is what is this? What is its purpose? When was it made? Is it easy to make?”

There was another moment of silence before the helmet said “Item is a simple combination of various elements and plastic compounds that has been formed using an unknown manufacturing process into a flexible rope-like material. It has been further formed into a wrist bracelet for decorative purposes. It is very long-lasting and will stay relatively stable for several millennia. Carbon-dating of traces in the fibers of the material indicates that the base material was made approximately twenty-five to twenty-seven centuries ago. The process to make this material is un-documented and therefore unavailable to retrieve.”

Both of our jaws dropped at the mention of when the material was made but that made absolutely no sense.

Mrs. Lambskin quickly asked “When were the components first discovered?”

The flat reply from the helmet was “The compound based on phenol-formaldehyde was discovered in the year 1909 of the pre-upheaval era and first mass-produced starting in the year 1910 of the pre-upheaval era.”

I chimed in at this point “So if we assume that that compound was made in the year 1910, and that this bracelet’s material is over 2500 years old, that means that right now, it is the year 4410 using the old dating method?”

Mrs. Lambskin jumped in with asking "When did the Great Upheaval occur in the old era?"

That unnervingly flat voice answered "According to the abstract of the paper titled 'Reconstruction of the events of The Great Tectonic Shift of 2047 and Subsequent Implications for the Human Race' published in the year 2059 Old Era by Vasquez, Tshombe, and Al-Naemi, the geological and political cataclysm that has become to be known as The Great Upheaval occurred in the year 2047 of the old era. It began with a massive 9.2 earthquake just off the North American Pacific coast centered between Whidbey Island and the town of Port Townsend in the state of Washington at approximately 7:42am on August 11. The South Whidbey Island fault subsided taking most of Whidbey Island and northern portions of the Olympic Peninsula into the ocean. The initial tsunami that was generated reached in excess of two-hundred-thirty-two feet in height and washed away virtually everything up to sixty-two miles inland. Two days of aftershocks measuring from 4.7 to 6.2 on the Richter Scale caused more subsidence of the land mass around the northern edge of what was termed the Cascades Subduction Zone, along with further tsunamis that combined to finish the devastation started with the initial earthquake and tsunami. Approximately 6.2 million of the estimated 6.3 million people, or roughly ninety-eight percent of the then population in the greater Puget Sound area, perished in the initial quake and the aftershocks."

Both of us were just hanging on every word since obviously neither of us had ever heard this version of our history before. I don't think *anybody* had ever heard this before, to tell the truth. I was fascinated because I had never heard this so-called official recounting before, while Mrs. Lambskin was starting to look pale.

The voice kept on its monotonic narration "The United States of America declared the area a disaster zone and rushed thousands of people to the area to look for and assist any survivors since all electricity and water distribution systems were destroyed or otherwise made inoperable. However, approximately 62 hours after the initial earthquake, the continental shelf of Northwest North America further shifted and the ancient Yellowstone caldera erupted in a magnitude 8.7 earthquake, magma, and ash event. The center third of the North American continent was buried in ash ranging in depth from several inches to over three feet. Virtually all of the crops being grown in that area perished within days. This eruption and subsequent aftershocks killed an additional forty-six million people. While most of the world's focus was on this disaster, within six days of the Yellowstone eruption several other countries decided to take advantage of the situation and launched their muon and neutron weapons at the United States and various other nations and coalitions around the world in an attempt to take over the world's dominion."

I was getting lost in the details here but Mrs. Lambskin evidently was feeling it more since she now had tears forming in her eyes.

"Stop! Enough already!" cried Mrs. Lambskin, and she was really crying. Water was literally pouring out of her eyes, down the valley between her nose and cheeks, and dripping off her chin.

"Are you ok?" I timidly asked.

"I'll be fine, just give me a minute or two" she replied as she walked over to the corner of the room and stood with her back to me.

While she was composing herself, my mind was spinning like our wind-turbines do when it gets breezy around here. "If the Great Upheaval was in the year 2047 of the Old Era and if we add our era's year of 1637, since we started counting again from the point of the Great Upheaval, that means in the old years it is the year 3684. But on the other hand, if the bracelet was made somewhere after 1910 and it is about 2500 years old, then it means it *really* is somewhere around the year 4410 using the old counting. That means, oh my goodness, 4410 minus 3684 gives us more than a *seven-hundred-year* gap between the Great Upheaval and when we started counting years? That can't be right, can it? When did our ancestors actually start counting the years again?"

She turned to me and said "You're right. For over seven-hundred years, there is no recorded history."

I was really beginning to hate that helmet, for what it had just told us, as well as for what it chimed in with at that moment. It hadn't turned off when Mrs. Lambskin stopped its previous narration, but had evidently switched into 'listen' mode and decided to rectify her erroneous last statement.

"Correction, there are records available of the seven-hundred and fifty-two years between the Great Cataclysm and what is commonly accepted as the start of the current era. What do you wish to know about?"

"Just stop, we don't want to hear anymore" she hoarsely yelled back at the poor machine. "My goodness, my goodness" is all she could say before she turned to me again. "You are never to tell anyone about this, you hear me? NEVER! We have made a new world without any of the hatred of the old world, no more wars, no more fighting for anything that one person has and another person wants. We've learned to share; share our world and share our thoughts instead of putting up walls around our fragile egos and never admitting that we might be wrong in our thinking and reasoning. We have built something very special for all our people and we all deserve a chance to make it the best world we can live in, so you are never to repeat to anyone anything that you have heard here about our past." Then she turned away from me and said solemnly "I need to be alone for a bit so its time you go. Come back in an hour or so and we'll get back to our immediate problem" and then she went to her room and closed the door behind her.

* * *

I left but my mind was still churning as I walked away towards my house. I just couldn't believe it – nothing survived the Great Upheaval, or so we thought, and so the school taught us. It was mind-bendingly overwhelming to find this story buried in so simple an artifact as my bracelet. Over seven-hundred years were missing from our history and I knew I needed to know sooner or later just what had happened during that period.

* * *

I returned to Mrs. Herula's house after that hour had passed.

Mrs. Lambskin met me at the front door, a whole lot more composed than when I left her, and she asked "Does your father have any more of this material? I'd like to see it if I can."

"Honestly, I don't know, but we can take a walk over to my house and ask him. Oh shoot, he got taken to the jail by Mr. Bacon. Do you think he'll let us talk to my Dada?"

"He's going to now; I'll make sure of that" Mrs. Lambskin said emphatically.

We both got up quickly and went out the door. It took about five minutes for us to walk over to Mr. Bacon's house since he made his front parlor into the official Sheriff's office.

"Yes, what is it?" said Mr. Bacon after we walked into his parlor. He was sitting there at his sheriff's desk in the corner of the room reading today's 'Sultanawash Herald', all five pages-worth of our local newspaper.

"We need to talk to Mr. Raindrum Whitehorse" said Mrs. Lambskin quickly. "It's important."

"I'm not sure I can let EG talk to him but I guess if the Deputy Prosecutor is going to be there; you *are* going to be there with him…?" Mr. Bacon asked.

"Yes, it'll be the two of us. Don't worry; I won't let the two of them talk privately" Mrs. Lambskin replied.

“What’s this about? Something I need to know about as Sheriff?” Mr. Bacon continued as he switched into his official voice.

“It’s a little detail that might lead us to who the real culprit is, but we do need to talk to him as soon as possible” Mrs. Lambskin urged. “Don’t worry, anything that he tells us I’ll gladly let you know, after all, I am the Deputy Prosecutor in this case and the one who ultimately is in charge of the investigation.”

“Yeah, yeah, yeah… ok, I’ll walk you over there. But you just make sure that you tell me anything that’s pertinent.”

At that, Mr. Bacon carefully folded the newspaper, got up, stretched a bit, and we headed out. He sure didn’t appear to have been getting either much rest or much exercise lately because before we walked five minutes, he was already wheezing a bit. But we got to the jail and I saw that Dada was just sitting in the tent I had pitched off to the side of the official jail building; sitting cross-legged with his eyes closed and his hands on his knees. When I called “Dada?” it still took a couple moments before his eyes opened and a grin spread across his face as he saw me.

Chapter 12 - *Some Light Starts Showing*

"I'm glad to see you, son" Dada said as he stood up and hugged me. "Why is she here?" he asked more formally as his gaze wandered to Mrs. Lambskin.

"I'm here because I need to do some more investigation into this whole fiasco" was Mrs. Lambskin's even reply. "Some things just don't add up and since I know you didn't murder those people, and I'm pretty sure your son Eaglefeeder didn't either, we need to look deeper into this."

"Just as long as you believe EG didn't do it and aren't trying to find some critical piece of evidence to pin it on him, I'm ok with answering whatever you want to ask. Otherwise, I'll stick to my story and tell anyone who wants to know that I did it." My father looked Mrs. Lambskin directly in the eyes as he said this quite firmly.

"Dada, I know you didn't do it just as well as I know I didn't do it, so could you help us by telling us where the material for our bracelets came from? Do you have a stash of it somewhere?" I pleaded with him.

"Yes, Mr. Whitehorse, I believe the key to this whole mystery is that bracelet and since you and your son are the only ones in this town who wear this specific one, it must mean that someone has somehow figured out how to either make a copy or have found the material somewhere where it's been hidden" Mrs. Lambskin said.

"Wellll," Dada drawled out, "According to our family's traditions I'm not supposed to divulge the location where that material is kept, but in this case, I guess it's best to just show you."

"I don't think Mr. Bacon is going to let you walk out of here, so you're just going to have to tell us", was Mrs. Lambskin's quick reply. Dada started to say something more but then she thought about it for another second and then said "Well, I don't see why you can't be released in my custody, after all, I'm a Deputy Prosecutor which means I am also an Officer of the Law. But before I go back to see him, I need to know more about this material. Where does it come from and how do you know how to make the bracelet for starters."

Dada frowned a bit and then said "This is part of our family and not for everyone to know. It's a part of being a Whitehorse, it's part of who we are as a family going back many, many generations" and he paused, then continued with "Well, I guess I can tell you, both of you, but both must solemnly swear that you will not divulge any of the story to anyone else", then looked directly at me and said "I mean it, son. You must never tell any of your friends or anyone else until you at least get married. The tradition is that the men in the family don't get let in to the secret until they get married to a woman. After that, you can only let your wife know until and if you have a son, and then only when he gets to be twelve years old. There is only one way out of this tradition, or promise if you will, and that is if the father gets sick and is possibly going to die. Then he can pass the tradition on to anyone else in his family but only after extracting this very same promise; that you will never let it out of the family. Do you understand, son?"

I looked at Dada square in the eyes and solemnly said "I promise."

Mrs. Lambskin jolted this tense exchange with "But what if a male doesn't get married to a woman, or doesn't get married at all, or if they don't have a son for a child?"

"The Whitehorse family, for as long as can be remembered, has always had a son in each generation. Don't ask me why or how this happens; it just does" was my father's terse reply.

"That doesn't make any sense," Mrs. Lambskin muttered, then said "but we really need to know about this bracelet" and then when she caught Dada looking at Mr. Bacon, she turned and said to him "I don't think we need you around right now; I can vouch for Mr. Whitehorse not running away or anything."

Mr. Bacon gave all three of us a good looking-over, grunted, and started walking back in the direction of his house.

"Okay, nobody else is around. *What is the secret of that material*?" Mrs. Lambskin firmly whispered to my father.

My father got a little grin on his face, beckoned a finger at us, and began walking out of the jail enclosure towards our house. We got there about five minutes later and he abruptly stopped. “Once again, whatever you see does not go any further, okay?” he said.

Mrs. Lambskin nodded and said “*Okay* already; let’s get going.”

Dada led us around the back of our house into the small grove of trees that were behind the house. After another two or three minutes he stopped and pointed to the trap door leading into our root cellar. We really didn’t use it that much anymore except for storage of odds and ends since we got that freezer in the kitchen a couple years back. He twisted the locking wire off, pulled open the door, and started down the twelve steps into the cellar. We both followed him and he clicked on the light powered by the solar cell on the house roof. Yep, there was that old baby crib covered by that plastic sheet, the small whiteboard that I used to draw pictures on with the markers, a couple old hand saws, and some other stuff that I had forgotten about since it had been at least a year or two since I’d been down there.

Dada took about ten steps over to the back wall and pushed aside a piece of lumber that appeared to be holding up the ceiling rafters but obviously was a fake, then twisted and pushed the door handle that had been concealed. There was a loud groan and the back wall of the cellar opened up. I had never seen this before even though I had spent quite some time down here goofing around when I was just a little kid; heck, I had occasionally invited Glukey and Sukey down here when we were little and none of us ever found this secret door.

Dada stooped a little and walked down a couple stairs into the room that was revealed and Mrs. Lambskin and I followed without a word. He reached off to his left and snapped on another light switch to reveal a room about as big as the root cellar, but perfectly clean; no dust anywhere. The walls looked to be made of concrete and very strong, also very old. On one wall I could just barely make out a faded 'CD' in a triangle painted on the wall, but there were no other real markings to indicate what this room was originally for.

Mrs. Lambskin beat me to the punch by asking "What is this room?"

"I'm not really sure what this was at one time, but my father brought me in here when I was twenty-two and showed me a couple things," Dada said. "For instance, this here box thing", indicating a small shoebox-sized metal cube with a switch and dial on top, "is a meter that measures how much radiation there is around. My father said a long, long time ago people needed to use one of these regularly but as far as he knew, that practice stopped back before his grandfather's time." He picked it up and flipped the switch on top of the box, there was a brief crackle type noise and the little needle on the dial flickered a little. "I guess people just didn't need it anymore" Dada said as he put it down. "This thing over here is a personal transportation thing" he said as he pointed at a small flat board thing with small wheels on the bottom. "Supposedly, all you had to do was switch it on like this" and he flicked another switch on the side of it, "then stand on it and lean whichever way you wanted to go and it would zoom you off until you straightened up and then it would stop. But, as you can see, whatever powered it doesn't work anymore" as he stood on it and leaned forward.

Mrs. Lambskin was getting antsy while I was just looking around at the odd stuff that was there and she abruptly said "Okay, this is all fine. Relics from the old ages, *but what about that cloth*?"

Dada walked over to another metallic box more in the corner and said "This is what you're looking for. There are these containers over there" as he pointed behind the machine, "that are connected with hoses to this thing. You turn on the switch and it asks you what you're looking to make and for these bracelets you just type in 'Whitehorse bracelet'. Here, let me show you" as he flicked on the switch labeled 'power'. The machine beeped once and on the small screen was the question "Enter desired material". Also, on the bottom of the screen was displayed a keyboard just like the Micoazanon console in the town hall. Dada typed in 'Whitehorse bracelet' and a whine from the machine started, then grew a bit louder. There were also some noises from the containers behind and within about a minute, a door opened on the side of the box and a piece of the bracelet material about eight inches long slid out down the chute to the tray on the side.

Mrs. Lambskin picked up the bracelet and asked my father "Does anyone else know of this machine or how you get the material for the bracelet?".

"As far as I know, your mother and I are the only ones that know about this machine" was Dada's response as he looked at me. "It wouldn't do the town's cloth factory any good if anyone found out about this machine that probably can make any clothing material in any quantity whenever anyone wants; that's why it's a secret kept within our family."

"Is it possible that there are other machines like this around here somewhere?" asked Mrs. Lambskin with a bit of a frown on her face.

"You know, that's funny you should ask" replied my father with a sudden odd look on his face. "I vaguely remember my grandfather saying something like that someone else in Sultanawash had one of these machines, but I was only five or six years old at the time and really can't remember any specifics."

"But Dada, you never showed me the machine until just now and I'm seventeen years old, so you were shown the machine when you were just five?" I butted in with, feeling a bit let-down about it.

"Well, EG, my father got real sick when I was like I say, five or six years old and my grandfather was afraid that my Dada wouldn't be around to teach me about our family tradition and grandpa knew he wouldn't be around for many more years, so he brought me down here and showed it all to me then. Dada eventually got better after about another month or two, and grandpa I guess was relieved that he wouldn't have to teach me about our family and he passed on shortly after Dada got better. I guess grandpa told Dada about telling me because it was about a year or so later, when I was about seven years old, that my Dada took me down here and showed it all to me and explained the family secret. I have nothing against you EG, I just never got around to showing you, I mean, I never considered the machine as that important, only for making the bracelet while it was the actual passing on of our family's heritage and traditions that really counted."

I have to confess, I was a bit let-down by Dada's apparent rudeness towards me, but I figured it as later better than never finding out about the actual machine.

Mrs. Lambskin pulled us both back out of our 'family talk' by asking "So, if there was another one of these machines in Sultanawash at one time, how do we find out if and where it was located, and further, who it belonged to?"

Dada had this look on his face like when he was trying to figure out which way the mountain goat was going to go next that last time he took me out hunting when Mrs. Lambskin asked "Are there any relatives of yours in Sultanawash? Did your parents ever tell you about someone else from your family living around here?"

"I wonder," Dada started with, paused, then continued with "I vaguely remember Grandpa talking a couple times about the Slowhawk family; how he used to hang around with a girl named LaughingDeer Slowhawk when he was a little boy, but something uh," and he paused for a second, "uh, happened when he was just seven years old. Maybe they had one of these machines also, I mean, just the names sound like someone from our old clan, or am I just reaching?"

"Hmm, LaughingDeer Slowhawk. I have to admit it does sound like someone from a family heritage like yours" said Mrs. Lambskin, "but it might be nothing at all."

"Why don't we just ask the machine?" I jumped in with, "after all, it seems to be connected into the Micoazanon helmet system, so maybe it knows?"

Both Mrs. Lambskin and Dada turned to me with expressions of 'I never thought of that' on their faces, and then Mrs. Lambskin went to the machine and typed in "What machine is this?".

Almost instantaneously, the screen lit up and displayed "Model AXP-47 controller for Garnerelle MJ9 cloth synthesizer; serial number A-479324g; currently connected to Micoazanon systems at port 26".

"So, it *is* connected to Micoazanon" she murmured as she next typed in "Model AXP-47 controllers in Sultanawash?"

The screen went dark for an instant, then displayed a list with two locations – one was listed as "Whitehorse family, 248 Cedar Lane Sultanawash" but the other was "Slowhawk family, 872 Alder Street Sultanawash".

"So," Mrs. Lambskin announced with a big smile on her face "we have another one of these machines in Sultanawash and consequently another source for this bracelet, which in turns means that it is possible that someone else made one of these bracelets and therefore it isn't certain that EG did the murders."

"Uhh," Dada butted in with, "but there isn't a Slowhawk family in Sultanawash or anywhere near here, at least not that I remember, your grandfather's friend and her family all perished in the thirty-year-flood of 1609, twenty-eight years ago, and Alder Street doesn't exist anymore."

"Why didn't you say that at first? You first said just 'something happened' and now it turns out they're all dead!" barked Mrs. Lambskin.

"I don't like talking about bad things happening, just let it go" was Dada's firm response.

Chapter 13 – *Search for The Machine*

I, along with Mrs. Lambskin, just stared at Dada after that comment. The look on Mrs. Lambskin's face had quickly changed from triumph after finding out about another possible machine, to despair after Dada's comment.

"Well, look at it this way then. If there was a machine like this in Sultanawash at one time, maybe it's still here somewhere" I said. "It gave us an address, so let's go over there and look for it, right?"

Mrs. Lambskin immediately brightened up and replied "You're absolutely correct. Let's go over there right now. It said the address was 872 Alder Street, right?" and she immediately turned to head for the stairs out of the cellar.

"But I just told you Alder Street doesn't exist anymore" pleaded Dada.

"Well, you know where it was don't you?" was Mrs. Lambskin's quick retort.

"Yeah, well kinda. It ran parallel to Elm Street about two or three blocks away near the northern cliff, but most of that area washed away in the flood we had. I was just a kid at that time and geezo did it rain and rain for at least three weeks without letup. Then we got these really big winds blowing through; I thought our house was going to be blown away. Well anyway, when the weather finally cleared up a bit, the town postman at that time, I think his name was Mr. Garuda, reported that a whole couple blocks of Sultanawash just weren't there anymore."

We grabbed some pruning shears and a flashlight since Dada thought we might need them if the area was overgrown with plants, then started walking towards the north end of Sultanawash and after about fifteen minutes Dada stopped and said "I think this is about where Alder Street was" as he pointed towards a small grove of willow trees. We all paused to look over the area, looking for any signs of houses or buildings. It was kind of a wild area, overgrown with berry bushes intertwined around the scraggly willow trees and lots of wild ferns. I all of a sudden had this strange feeling that we were being watched but just put it off as being in a part of town that nobody goes near anymore because of the deaths that had occurred here during that flood.

"Well, where do we go from here?" I asked Mrs. Lambskin.

"Let's see if we can find any signs of the street like maybe power lines or paving and go from there" she replied with a hopeful look on her face.

It took the three of us about twenty minutes to find a piece of that black-tar paving and then another couple minutes to find an old mailbox with 803 painted on its side, so we knew we were in the right area. Another ten or so minutes and we found a chunk of what must have been a house wall and another couple minutes later Dada found a set of mailboxes still attached to a post. We were all getting pretty scratched up by the berry bushes and a bit disheartened until we looked at those mailboxes and sure enough, one of them had '872' painted on the side along with a little painting of a hawk in flight, so we knew we were looking in the right area. Now the only problem was to find where the actual house was since those ganged-up mailboxes could have been twenty feet away from the Slowhawk house or they could have been a hundred feet away. But, like I said, we were in the right area. It was difficult terrain though; you could still see big gullies here and there where the flood waters had gushed through almost thirty years ago.

"I'm thinking that the Slowhawks would have had that machine in a cellar or outbuilding like you have" said Mrs. Lambskin, "so, since there aren't many pieces of buildings left around here, let's see if we can find some kind of cellar door out back of where the actual house would be like you people have."

We still had a lot of ground to cover and it was at least an hour later that Mrs. Lambskin actually tripped and fell down on top of what looked like a cellar door. "I think I found something" she called to Dada and me. We must have spent another ten minutes or so clipping berry bushes and vines out of the way before we could get the door open. Just like Mrs. Lambskin thought, it was a setup very similar to our house and cellar. We went down the steps and Dada eagerly showed the light around.

The room was completely barren; there were just four bare walls, a floor, and nothing else.

I learned a couple new curse words in the next few moments as Mrs. Lambskin let loose with a couple good ones (like 'com-boosha' which was one I had actually heard before from old Amboy when Mrs. Jeronas' goat had just peed on him, which is also why I knew Mrs. Lambskin was cursing, but 'bee-eff-eff it!' was a new one) before she finally calmed down a bit after Dada broke into her rant with "There's probably a secret door here just like our cellar so let's look around." Sure enough, it only took about two minutes to find the door and the release lever. We walked down the next set of steps and sure enough, there was the same setup as our little room. There were quite a few little odds and ends down there, but there wasn't a cloth synthesizer.

We looked all around as Mrs. Lambskin started muttering more curse words but that thing just wasn't there anywhere. We even searched the walls to see if there was another door to another room but came up short; there just wasn't anything there. It was only as we were walking out of the room that I saw something on the floor; a piece of cloth with green and red interwoven threads. I picked it up and said "Well, that machine must have been here at one time because here's a piece of cloth just like our bracelets" as I showed it to the others. "The colors are different but if you compare it to our bracelets, the actual cloth looks pretty much the same."

Mrs. Lambskin was still quite grumpy and snapped "Yeah, but that still doesn't feed the bulldog. We got to find that machine because then we know who has it or used it last, and if we find that person, we can then find out if they made a bracelet like yours, and if they did, then we know that there is a good possibility that you or your father didn't kill those kids."

She was right of course; finding that little scrap of cloth didn't really solve anything but the question of whether or not we had the only machine that could make our bracelets. We took the little scrap with us when we left the hidden room and the unused cellar. As Dada was refastening the cellar door Mrs. Lambskin suddenly asked "Who else knew the Slowhawk family? Maybe we can find someone else that knew them and perhaps knew about the machine. What do you think?" she said as she looked at Dada.

"Oh, that narrows the field down quite a bit" he snickered "since pretty much everyone in this town knows everyone else in it." And then he got a serious look on his face and said "Well, come to think of it, the Railsfords used to live up here somewhere maybe a block or three away, and moved down closer to our house after that flood as a precaution if it ever flooded again. I remember I was about six or seven and very happy that I had a new playmate in Joram Railsford, Glukey's father, living only a block or two away."

"Hmm, sounds like a clue that maybe we should follow up on" said Mrs. Lambskin.

"But, but, Glukey couldn't have done it; he adored Amber!" I shouted.

"Yes, but we have to explore the coincidence of the Railsfords living near the only other family in Sultanawash that have one of those fabric machines, and the fact that two Railsfords were at the camp when the murders were committed" said Mrs. Lambskin firmly. "I know it's a bit of a stretch knowing Glukey and Sukey, but it's still an interesting coincidence."

We headed back towards our house and I didn't say a whole lot because I just couldn't believe Glukey could or would do a thing like killing another person, especially Amber who he liked so much. Dada and Mrs. Lambskin didn't say much either on that walk home but I could tell both of them were also thinking hard about the possibilities.

* * *

It was already getting dark by the time we got back to our house. Mrs. Lambskin had decided that we still needed to talk more about the case which was why she didn't immediately escort Dada back to Mr. Bacon's jail.

"Well, what have we got to show for our little adventure? One small piece of cloth and nothing else, so now what?" I asked as Dada climbed into his favorite sitting chair, the one that vibrates and heats up in the winter.

"What we have is proof that another cloth-making machine exists or at least existed in Sultanawash, which means that it's still entirely possible that someone made a bracelet just like yours so they could murder those three kids and have you blamed for it; that's what we've got" snapped Mrs. Lambskin.

"Okay, so what if there is that someone else around here that made a bracelet like ours. How do we find them without having to go search every house in Sultanawash?" asked Dada a bit peeved himself. I could sense that he was getting a big ragged around the edges himself mainly because if we couldn't find anyone else with that bracelet material either him or I would get convicted of killing Amber, Jellie, and Dorman and get sent away to McNeil Island for the rest of our life.

"Well, wait a minute. Those bracelets you both wear; can you take them off or are they permanently stuck on your wrists?" asked Mrs. Lambskin as if a burst of light had gone off in her head.

"No, they're permanently stuck on our wrists, at least I think it's permanent. I've never even thought of taking it off ever since my father put it on" said Dada as he started pulling on his bracelet. "Yeah, see? It won't stretch enough to be able to pull it off and it definitely won't just break; you'd have to take a knife or something to it" he continued as he kept fiddling with his bracelet.

"Well here, let me see something. Hold out your arm," said Mrs. Lambskin as she reached over to grab his hand. She held onto his hand with one hand and started pulling at the bracelet with her other hand.

"Hey, stop that!" yelped Dada as he tried to pull his hand away. "Now look at what you did" as he managed to yank his wrist away from her. "My wrist is all raw now from you yanking on it."

"That's just what I was thinking would happen" she responded. "If someone else was wearing a bracelet like this and started pulling on it to take it off, their wrist would get rubbed raw. So, all we have to do is gather up everyone that was out there and look at their wrists to see which one has a chafed wrist" she proclaimed proudly.

"Yeah but," I interrupted, "what if they didn't fasten it on like Dada did with a candle flame?"

Dada also chimed in with "Oh come on now, that was almost three weeks ago. You don't expect someone to still be walking around with a chafed wrist? It must have healed over by now, especially if they used pine-needle balm on it."

I could see those remarks didn't sit well with Mrs. Lambskin because her previous frown returned. "Well, it's something to look for at least" she finally sputtered out.

***

It was almost an hour later that she was finally able to get all the people that were out at camp, and Mr. Bacon, over to her house. Mrs. Lambskin, once everyone was all crowded into Mrs. Herula's living room, finally said "I've called you all here because we have found new evidence that may impact the case in hand. I want all of you to think about that vision you all had at Jellie Overholser's memorial ceremony. You all saw her being stabbed by someone holding a knife in their hand, right?" There was a murmur of agreement from everyone at her question. She continued with "Now, I know it'll be difficult and maybe painful to remember, but what did the hand look like? Was it small? Large? Tanned? White? Timtim, tell me what you see."

He probably wasn't a good choice by Mrs. Lambskin to start things off but oddly enough Timtim replied clearly "I dunno, maybe it was a small white hand holding the knife, uhh, maybe not; is that what you want me to say?"

WassaJo both responded to that with "That's what we saw, too", as did Glukey and Elnor.

Mrs. Lambskin looked to Aku, Sansa, and Sukey to find out what they remembered and gave a little gasp.

Chapter 14 – *The Confession*

I have to say, people in Sultanawash generally go about their days with, I can't say a smile on their face, but generally a look like there's not much troubling them at all. I mean, they don't walk around frowning or snarling like a hungry coyote, but what I saw at that moment was enough to freeze the pee out of my bladder.

Mrs. Lambskin focused in on Sukey who was looking as if she had just put her hand in a pot of boiling stew and asked gently "Suukkeey? Is there something you want to say?"

That evidently wasn't quite the right question to ask Sukey because Sukey immediately exploded with "You think you're on to something Mrs. Know-It-All? Well, lemme tell you what all your poking and prying has done for this town and everybody that lives in it. You can't just leave us to live the lives we want to live, ohh nooo! You got to get everyone riled up and looking at everyone else in a bad way and, and…" and then she spluttered out and just started crying.

"Sukey, what's wrong?" asked Glukey earnestly.

"Oh, just leave me alone, will you? First, you start being real friendly towards Amber and then, then EG starts up with Jellie and, and, nobody has any time for me anymore!" she finally spit out. "Even Lackey makes fun of me all the time just because I like EG."

“Sukey, hush, hush” Glukey tried as he had his arms around her. “Nobody is making fun of you. So what if you like EG, a lot of us do.”

Elnor broke in at this moment with “So YOU’RE the one that killed Amber, Jellie, and Dorman!”

Glukey immediately turned on Elnor and barked “How DARE you say such a thing? You’re the one that’s all gas and pimples with everyone else! YOU’RE the one that is always yelling at people for just doing what they do! How do we know that you didn’t kill those three just because they weren’t good enough for you?”

In the meantime, Aku had paled and stuck her face into TimTim’s chest with this exchange. WassaJo were just sitting there with faces that looked like they had just eaten some really hot peppers. Mr. Bacon had this look of “what do you expect me to do?” on his face while Mr. Jivey just looked completely lost again. Of all of them, Sansa was the only one who looked like this was something she expected which was confirmed when she said defiantly “I knew it had to be one of us; there just wasn’t any other idea that made any sense but I thought it was Dorman, that is until he got killed too.”

“Why the heck would you think Dorman was the one? On a good day, Dorman couldn’t fry an egg without asking how!” yelled Elnor.

“Well, Dorman was always going around showing how strong he was and…” Sansa started.

“Yeah but, Dorman wasn’t the brightest guy around, that’s for sure” retorted Elnor. “Plus, he was a really nice guy that would always help you out, just as long as you had the patience to explain just exactly what you wanted him to help you with. I can’t tell you how many times he helped me out around the house when I had things to do…”

“Yeah, so you liked him a lot; you were sweet on him, right?” Sansa came back with as her temper started to flare.

After Sansa’s earlier comment about not liking Elnor, I wasn’t surprised by her latest comment, but you know, up to that specific day, I don’t think I ever saw Elnor blush. Oh, she would get all high and mighty on occasion when she was telling you just what was the right thing to do, or the right way to do something, but I had never seen her get red in the face before. Even that time Sukey tried playing a trick on her with that dead snake in Elnor’s lunch pail, I had never seen Elnor get embarrassed. Now, the room seemingly lit up with how bright red her face was.

“Oho, so you got mad at him for something and took the occasion to kill him?” Sansa just would not let it go.

Elnor just sat there and started crying, another thing I had never seen before from her.

“Wait a minute! How do we know it wasn’t little miss know-it-all Sansa?” exploded Glukey. “You were always butting in on everyone else’s conversations as if you knew everything already! You’re the one that’s always trying to make herself look important!”

"I am not a butt-insky!" barked Sansa. "I just want everyone to know I'm here and worth something. My parents sure don't seem to care a whole lot whether I'm alive or …" she trailed off as she started crying.

I looked around and between people crying and yelling at each other, I was completely flabbergasted as to who did what or even what actually happened. I mean, this was completely opposite of our usual days in Sultanawash where people just went about their days doing what they normally did. All I can say is that the only thing I really knew was that I didn't do it, whatever 'it' was at the moment. I didn't call anyone any names, I didn't badmouth anyone behind their back, and I sure didn't murder anyone. But everything else, I guess, was up to debate.

"Wait a minute, just wait a minute!" bellowed Mrs. Lambskin. Everyone else either shut up or stopped crying at that moment, even Mr. Bacon came out of his brain fog and looked at Mrs. Lambskin.

"Sukey, did you kill Amber, Jellie, and Dorman?" she asked firmly.

"OF COURSE I DID!" yelled Sukey. "All of you just going along with everything the old people say" she shouted at the rest of us kids, "and no thought at all to what WE might want to do. WE might want to go and have fun for a change! WE might want to go and make our own rules! WE might want to go and, and, and kiss whoever we want to kiss when we want instead of that old witch Mrs. DeAngelo telling us we're going to burn in hell forever, and, and…" she finally stopped and just put her hands to her face and started crying.

I was completely dumbfounded by Sukey's affirmation that she killed Amber, Jellie, and Dorman. It was all I could do to remain standing because all I wanted to was faint and fall down. "No, this can't be true" is what raced around and around in my mind like Mr. Legaspi's goofy dog after he tried eating some blackberries off the vine and got a thorn in his mouth. Everyone else in the room was shocked beyond belief. After a few seconds, Mr. Bacon finally stirred, cleared his throat, and mumbled "Sukey, I'm afraid I have to take you to jail. Please don't make this any harder than it already is." He stepped towards Sukey as she just stared at him and grasped her by the wrist.

"Hold on a second, Mr. Bacon" said Mrs. Lambskin. "I don't know if I want to believe Sukey could have killed those other three kids. I want to hear her story before you take her away. After all, maybe she did, and just maybe she's covering for someone else like Eaglefeeder's father was doing when he confessed that day in court."

Mr. Bacon paused and again mumbled "Fine, I'm not sure I can walk over to the jail just yet anyway. Her confession kinda hit me a bit hard. I've listened to people admitting they ate more than their fair share for dinner, or that they tried to gather all the mushrooms before anyone else could get there, but nothing like this, Lord knows, nothing like this" and he sat back down with a 'whumpf' but still kept his hold on Sukey's wrist.

"Sukey? What happened out there at the camp? Tell us just what you did" said Mrs. Lambskin in a firm voice. "What happened that first night?"

Sukey had by now quieted back down. She looked around at the rest of us who were all waiting for her to say something, and finally started talking.

"I went to bed that first night with everyone else but I couldn't really sleep. I saw that Amber was watching the rest of us and when I faked falling asleep by making snoring noises, I saw her get up. I knew something was up because she was acting all sneaky. Then she crept over to the curtain and I could see her motioning to someone; I was pretty sure it was EG but she later said it was my brother Glukey but I doubt that. I don't know what came over me but I got so darn mad at her but then the alarm went off and everyone got up and started yelling. Finally, when Mr. Jivey quieted everyone down and we all went back to bed I decided that I wasn't going to let Amber try anything with EG."

At that, everyone looked at me and I was like "why me?" because I hadn't a clue up to that point that Sukey actually liked me that much. But then Sukey continued.

"All I could think of was somehow getting Amber out of the picture and then I remembered that when we first got to the camp and went in the bunkhouse, I saw this knife on a shelf next to my bed covered by a bunch of other things. Anyway, sometime after things quieted down, I got out of my bed and knelt next to Amber's bed. I shook her awake and asked her in a whisper why she was motioning to EG and she lied and said she wasn't; she was trying to get Glukey's attention. I told her I knew she was trying something with EG and she finally confessed that she was getting tired of Glukey and wanted to see if EG was interested in her. I guess that was it for me, I mean here was everyone's darling girl, the girl who was so nice and cute and honest and all that, and here she's really a liar and trying to take the guy that I'm interested in. And she was so smug about the whole thing like the world revolved around her and I lost my mind, grabbed the knife, and sliced across her throat."

That brought a very audible gasp out of everyone sitting there, I mean, I think everyone I knew in town was glad that Mr. Doncastle, the town butcher, did all the dirty work with the meat he sold so that none of us had to kill the animals involved. We, and I think I speak for pretty much the whole town, are not that comfortable at all with taking lives of any kind, and are truly glad that there are a few people like Mr. Doncastle that will do it for us.

Evidently, I was a bit mistaken about it because here was Sukey more or less matter-of-factly saying how she killed another person without much hesitation.

Mrs. Lambskin appeared quite shocked by Sukey's words, as did we all, but prodded Sukey again with "And then what happened with Jellie and Dorman?".

"So, I hid the knife under my cot and after a while fell asleep. Everything seemed to be ok after that except when we had Amber's memorial service, I could actually tell that EG only thought that Amber was a decent person; he really didn't have any feelings for her. It's funny but I could see that in my mind and tell that it came from EG, so that made me happier. But then there were other of EG's memories that I could see that were of Jellie and how he thought she was a good friend."

I butted in at that point and said "But I wasn't thinking of Jellie at Amber's ceremony so where did you get that idea?"

Mrs. Lambskin also appeared a bit confused by what Sukey said so she jumped in with "Can you see into people's minds? Even those things they aren't directly thinking about?"

"Yeah, if I concentrate hard enough, I can see pretty much anything in someone else's mind; they don't have to be actively concentrating on what I see because I can see most everything".

Mrs. Lambskin's reply was just "Fascinating; I've heard about a few people here and there that can see into other's minds but I never believed it, until now that is. And it seems like there are more and more of those reports happening. Fascinating, I wonder if we're all gradually turning into mind-readers, but if so…".

Mr. Bacon abruptly woke out of his stupor and barked "But SOOO WHAT??? Who cares about mind-reading; we got a person here that just confessed to killing another person. What're we going to do about that, HUH?"

"I just think it's fascinating that humans are evidently evolving faster than ever before…"

"Like I said, WHO GIVES A MELON BALL? We got a killer here that needs to be taken care of" roared Mr. Bacon.

"ALRIGHT ALREADY!" snapped Mrs. Lambskin at Mr. Bacon. "But I want to hear the rest of her story!" She turned back to Sukey and quietly asked "And then what happened with Jellie and Dorman?"

"After we had Amber's memorial service, I wasn't thinking a whole lot about anything. I mean, Glukey was pretty messed up about someone killing Amber so I was trying to get him calmed down. But then I saw Jellie go into the bathrooms and I just knew that I had to ask her whether she was serious about EG. I was also a bit afraid that she would find the knife that I had stashed in there earlier right before the memorial service, so I went in after her. I don't know how she did it but she found the knife somehow and I never got to ask her anything, things are a bit blurry from then on, but the next thing I remember is staring down at her as she was on the floor with the knife in her chest. I was a bit panicky but knew that I probably wouldn't be suspected of killing Jellie if I was the one who found her dead, so I called out to everyone else that I had found the knife."

As Sukey paused, I looked around at the others and everyone looked both angry and shocked at what Sukey had just said. I mean, she just said she killed someone in about the same tone as saying something like "I picked some cranberries for tonight's dinner". This was totally foreign to all of us; the thought that someone could so matter-of-factly admit to killing another person was, well, unbelievable.

Mrs. Lambskin then prodded Sukey again by asking "But what about the bracelet? Did you know about the fabric machine that the Slowhawks had hidden in their cellar? Where did that bracelet come from in the vision?" At that question, most everyone turned toward Mrs. Lambskin with a "what the heck?" look on their faces.

"There was no bracelet; I made that up in my memory" Sukey stated. "Jellie made me so mad when she laughed at the idea of me and EG – I guess that's what made me do it. But I got so mad at EG that it was pretty easy to make up that image of his hand with the bracelet on it stabbing her; I mean, all of us know about the bracelet."

"Fascinating; you can project your own thoughts and ideas to others" is what came out of Mrs. Lambskin's mouth at that point, but then she shook her head and asked "But what about Dorman?"

Sukey took a couple deep breaths and then continued with "Dorman? Some time after we did Jellie's memorial service, he asked me to walk with him because he had to talk to me. So, we walked around the back of the cabin and he told me that he noticed that I had some blood on my wrist when everyone crowded into the bathhouse and he wanted to know about it. I figured if he told anyone else about it, I would be suspected so I picked up a fair-sized branch and hit him in the face and then on top of his head and he went down. Next, I dragged him away from the cabin and threw a bunch of leaves on him so he wouldn't be found. Then I went back to the campfire circle and waited for everyone to come out of the cabin so I could quickly run back to where he was and drag him back into the cabin; I mean, I couldn't let some wild animal try to eat him, could I?"

That last statement of Sukey's really left us all pretty flabbergasted. I mean, here she deliberately killed someone and then was worried that some animal would start gnawing on his body? Yeesh, I don't know what exactly was going through Sukey's mind for the past week or couple months or for however long, but something wasn't quite right in her head, that was for sure. I'm also thinking that everyone else in that room at that moment was thinking pretty much the same as me about Sukey.

Mr. Bacon looked at Mrs. Lambskin at that point and growled "Can I FINALLY take her away now? I mean, you got whatever information you need and I think Sukey really needs to be put somewhere away from all of the rest of this town, so if it's all the same to you, I'm taking her to jail." He got up again and pulled Sukey along with him as he went out the front door. Like I said, everyone else was just pretty taken aback by what she had said, and I think also by how she said it.

Mrs. Lambskin finally stood up from her chair, murmured "So that fabric machine didn't have anything to do with it, but on the other hand, it had everything to do with it", and then straightened up and said to all of us remaining "You can all go now. I don't think there's anything anyone else can say that will change the fact that Sukey killed those three people and also that she's capable of doing it again, so thank you all for coming here but now, go home. I'll straighten things out in the morning with Mr. Bacon and Mr. Joniak and we'll make sure Sukey is taken care of. Now, like I said, go home; it's over."

At that point, as I filed out of Mrs. Herula's house with the rest of them, I didn't know what to think anymore. Over the past couple weeks, three people had been deliberately killed, I had been accused of that, my father tried to take the blame in my place, we went looking for and finally found evidence of someone else doing the killings, then found the cloth machine was a flying catfish because it didn't play into anything, yet it did ultimately lead to the true killer. Boy, my head was just swimming around and around and it's a miracle that I finally found my way back to my house. I knew it was going to take a lot of time before I could at last make some peace with it all.

But then, there were those nagging questions I had about what the Micoazanon helmet had told us, but I figured "Leave it alone" because it would just bring up more questions about who we all are and what we're all doing here. I was sure that I'd be talking to Mrs. Lambskin more in the coming weeks.

***

Thinking about all that happened last night at the house when I gathered together everyone involved, I am still a bit muddled in my thinking. I've got to make an official report of this whole case for our files but I'm just not sure where to start. I do think this has dampened my whole outlook on continuing as a Deputy Prosecutor but I need to put aside everything the helmet told us about the old ages and just concentrate on the fact that we found the killer of those three kids. So, I'll take what Sukey confessed to and see if I can put it into a description of 'this was the situation, this is what happened, and this is the outcome' and then have the other Deputies review it to make sure that it all makes sense.

I do think I'm going to stay around here in Sultanawash for a bit, not only to get the story put together, but also to just stay away from our office for a bit. But I think once I get done with pulling myself back together, I'll leave and hopefully never have to come back here again because I don't think I want or even can be reminded of this whole sordid affair. I need to get it out of my system and pick up my life, both personal and professional, where it was before I ever got involved in this mess. Here's where I end my part of the narrative, and I hope to high heaven I never have to even think about it again.

Chapter 15 – *Finally, Those Secrets I'll Take to My Grave*

Well, that's the story behind those killings as I and everyone else lived through it. I am now an old man, almost forty-eight years old, and probably can't count on more than another year or so, so I've been going through some of the stuff I've accumulated over my lifetime.

I've changed a lot since my younger days, those days that I've recounted in my journals under the heading "The Wilderness Camp Murders". I used to be I guess you'd call it nave, to use an ancient term for someone that really doesn't know or notice a whole lot that goes on around them. But what I learned from the helmet that I'll tell you about in a bit, and also just growing older, getting married, having a son, and being a part of the Sultanawash community over the past almost thirty years has given me some perspective on what I call life in general. That perspective is that people are innately good in their core and it's just circumstances that bend them one way or the other, towards being a good person or being a not-so-good person. For instance, Glukey, my best friend may he rest in peace, seemed to never be able to get over Amber's death and spent quite a few years moping around until he appeared to find some peace when he married Rajenee who sure enough did become Mayor. They had four children together and they really seemed to soothe any of his lasting grief over Amber. The rest of the group from that camp also seemed to get over those horrible couple weeks; for instance, Aku and Timtim got married eventually as did Josanna and Wassa and both couples lived happily until they passed on.

I know my end is close because I've been having those pains that Dada and Mama both had before they went to the hereafter. My joints, and even the bones themselves, are sore and stiff. There are times I can't catch my breath. I'm thirsty all the time even though I'm peeing constantly it seems. My stomach hurts like I need to eat something all the time even though most times the thought of eating makes me sick, and yesterday I coughed up a wad of blood. Dada, in his last couple months, seemed to all of a sudden get these ugly bruises all over and I've started noticing a couple on my arms and legs also even though I haven't really been doing a lot of anything. In the months before Mama left, she said that she was so very tired it was difficult to get out of bed in the morning. I've been doing a lot of sleeping-in myself these last couple weeks and it seems like there are times I just cannot get moving.

Anyway, enough of how I'm feeling these days. A couple weeks ago, I broke my promise that I made so many years ago to not use the Micoazanon helmet for anything other than ordering supplies, and asked what all this meant. The reply I got was the strong chance that I had blood and bone cancer with maybe another year or so of life left to me. I had figured as much before I even asked since the great majority of people around here don't live much past their forty-fifth birthday and a good number of those complain of more or less the same things that I'm suddenly experiencing.

I really don't want to saddle my son Greywolf, and especially my wife Lackey, bless her heart, with a lot of this old stuff, but most especially not these journals I've kept over the years. On the other hand, I am so accustomed to writing down things that have happened, my thoughts, and dealings with some of the people I've worked and lived with, that I still feel bound to continue. I will burn this when I think it's close to my time to pass on to the great beyond, both because there's a lot of things I've written down that won't possibly interest anyone else, and also because I have to write down what I discovered about Micoazanon and this world of ours. But then again, I don't want anyone else, nor should anyone else, ever find out The Big Secret of how this world of ours came to be. It may seem funny that I have to write this down just so I can burn it, but I really have to get this out of my mind, if for no other reason than to go to the great beyond with a clear conscience.

The only other person that knew some of the big secret, Geena Lambskin, passed on quite some years ago, and I still mourn her to this day. We did get to become pretty good friends after all that trial stuff finally got settled, and she was a good anchor for me – she kept me grounded. And, to my knowledge, she never went looking for the whole story of the old days and whenever I'd bring up the subject, she'd just reply "That was then, but this is now, so don't be poking around in things that happened so long ago that they really don't matter at all anymore." The one thing I especially remember Geena saying, the one thing that I know she believed in so much that she lived her life accordingly, is "It is up to us to make this world in whatever way we choose to live. I choose to live a good life, a life without constant struggles about one's ideas that one thinks are better than any other person's ideas; a life where everyone listens to and respects everyone else." I like that idea so much that I've tried my darndest to live that way for all my years.

I have never gotten over rambling all these years, so I need to get back to the subject at hand. I've never talked about this nor have I ever written anything down about it before, but it's time that I do write it down, if, like I said before, just to get it out of my head so I can spend the time I have left with some feeling of peace. It's been many years since I started writing these journals and as I look back over the thousands of pages I've written, I can see that I've changed from being that wide-eyed young man when I first started writing. I'm an old man now and have seen many things in my life, things that were just great like the birth of my son and his subsequent growth into a person that, upon reflection, does appear to have inherited quite a few traits from me. Now, I'm just tired all the time and hope a lot wiser than I once thought I was.

So, going back to those days of my youth, here's what happened.

The trial was over and everyone was feeling safe again now that we had finally figured out what happened to Amber, Jellie, and Dorman, yet the whole story seemed to leave a bad taste in many people's mouths. It took at least a month or two before the dark shadow that seemed to fall over us starting with Amber's death and ending with Sukey's banishment to McNeil Island, left Sultanawash completely. Mrs. Lambskin stayed at Mrs. Herula's house for a good four months more and we had occasional discussions, just the two of us, about what happened, the trial, and other stuff. Each time we talked the feeling that we were ignoring the grizzly bear in the corner grew until it seemed we couldn't ignore it any more.

Finally, 'that' conversation started with "EG, have you thought any more about what the helmet told us?" Mrs. Lambskin asked.

"What? You mean like when it gave us that story about how the Great Upheaval started and all that?" I responded.

"Exactly. Have you ever wanted to know the whole story or are you content now that it's all over, with just knowing a bit more than is taught in school?"

I have to admit, I bald-faced lied to her when I said "I think it's up to us to live the way we can and just forget about the past and the mistakes that were made back then." I really should have just told her I *had* to know, but I thought it would put her mind at ease if I just agreed with her viewpoint on the matter.

She more or less confirmed that I gave her the response she wanted to hear by responding "That's good. Even though someone way back once said 'those that cannot remember the past are doomed to repeat it', I think we have been given a chance to make a new way of life. I also think that we've pretty well succeeded with making a good life for everyone concerned. There is a time to think of what could have been done in certain situations but unless we carry those options in our mind and resolve to never make the same mistakes again, it all comes down to feeling guilty and that means that we're forever carrying that on our shoulders and not living the life that we could."

Geena had gotten pretty philosophical after what the helmet told us, and after going through the trial. I think it was because she was assuming some of that guilt that she was talking about. Me? I had heard the same things as she did but I wasn't about to let it run my life, especially since I saw how miserable she was by letting that knowledge just sit there and percolate through her mind over and over again like Mrs. Herula's ever-simmering coffeepot.

We talked many times over the next couple weeks and each time she started going back to the Great Upheaval and the devastation that followed, I would gently steer the conversation back to today's world, like preparations for Sultanawash's annual end of year celebration. That seemed to make a difference because after about three months she seemed perkier and mentioned all that stuff less and less. I could visibly see the difference in her; her mouth wasn't shaped into a frown all the time; her eyes got brighter; and her posture got straighter as if a great weight had finally slid off her shoulders.

* * *

I remember it was a couple weeks after Geena left to go back to her home in Wenatchawash that I couldn't stand it anymore. I've always been naturally curious about things that happen, not that I'm a gossip like Mrs. Angstrom who likes to snoop around and then tell absolutely everyone whatever she's stumbled on. There was that time that poor Dorman pinched a couple apples off of Mrs. Jeronas' apple tree and within a couple hours, everyone knew that he did it due to Mrs. Angstrom's well-maintained network. To get back to the point, I've always had a curiosity about things, like that machine that Dada showed us that made the bracelet. Anyway, I went and found a Micoazanon helmet and, after assuring myself that I'd have a good hour or two to myself, I nervously asked The Question.

"What happened after the war that started after the Great Upheaval?" I asked. The answer came swiftly.

That by-now well-known flat voice replied "The exchange of weapons that resulted from this initial attack lasted only four days before all war supplies were exhausted and more than ninety-two percent of the world's population, at that time totaling approximately eleven billion people, were dead or dying either directly from the explosions, or from the resultant radiation sickness from the neutron bombs. Further, the resultant concussions and shockwaves from using these weapons further destabilized sections of the earth's crust, resulting in additional plate migration, specifically the east side of the South American plate subsided with the North American plate, while the Eurasian and African plates rose over the next forty-two days. These tectonic shifts killed another estimated eight-hundred million people that otherwise had been relatively untouched in the nuclear exchange. In summary, of the world's estimated population of eleven billion people, as of two months after the Great Upheaval started with the Whidbey Island earthquake, there were only approximately eighty million survivors scattered around the world. Within a further nine months, the population of the world, as estimated by astronauts Hermann and Fontenoy who had been residents of the space station 'Peace' since two months before the cataclysm, was only six million due to the lasting effects of radiation and sudden climate shift brought on by the shifting of the earth's crust. The smoke from the continent of Australia which began burning en masse further contributed to the mini-ice age that ensued for the next three years before the previous climate patterns reasserted themselves."

There's a lot more I could tell you, things that the Micoazanon helmet told me about those 'missing' seven-hundred-odd years. How the human race almost completely perished from this planet, the part that those two astronauts orbiting the earth in that space station played in keeping this planet inhabited by things other than forests and animals before they died aboard the space station, how Doctors Vasquez, Tshombe, and Al-Naemi risked literally everything on the chance that Micoazanon would work, and so on. Even Micoazanon itself; we all had been taught that it was two of the largest corporations in the world that merged together. Nope, not even close to the truth. Yes, what we had today was the remnants of those two companies, along with a lot of other ones that more or less coalesced into one big company, but to call that company 'Micoazanon' was completely bogus.

Micoazanon was developed as a 'cure' for the radiation, disease, and famine sweeping the earth in the few short years after the event by Drs. Vasquez, Tshombe, and Al-Naemi.

With all the volcanoes erupting around the west coast of North and South America, most notably Mount Rainier and Mount Baker in what used to be Washington State, as well as the east coast of Asia, added to the fires from Australia, the exposed areas of the earth were blanketed in clouds of soot and ash that more or less killed most plants. The radiation present also suppressed anything living. What the doctors came up with was a fungus that stimulated growth in the new soil along with changing the genetic code of anything growing to accommodate the increased radiation. I'm not a scientist, nor would I ever want to be, and don't really understand what genetic coding really means but as I understand it, everything living including plants, animals, and people, have basic chemical compounds and structures in our bodies that regulate our growth and the doctors figured a way to revise those instructions so that we could thrive in our new world. They must have done a great job of it because everywhere you look or wander around, the plants and animals are all healthy and growing well. Outside of a few slightly bothersome things, like the lip diseases and the facial lesions that people occasionally get, people are all pretty healthy also. And one last interesting thing about Micoazanon is that it is still being continuously spread over the earth; it's in the fuel of those drones that are constantly flying around.

And about those big complexes the drones fly out of, satisfying our every needs, well, there aren't thousands of those complexes as Mr. Jorim claimed, there are only a couple dozen spread around the world. There just isn't enough people to staff any more than that, and really, their basic function was not to supply everyone left with whatever products they wanted or needed, it was to continually spread the Micoazanon dust throughout the world. It was just a convenient trick that the good doctors pulled on all of us to ensure that the dust would continue to be spread around the world so that the earth could heal itself and both plants and animals would continue to live. Having to distribute all kinds of goods to the remaining population around the world ensured that people would never shut down these complexes, so also making them the center for distributing Micoazanon dust was a clever ploy to ensure that the dust distribution would always continue. The various products that they are constantly delivering? Well, a good portion of them is made and come from the people around the world but the bigger more specialized stuff like those emergency generators we have come from pre-upheaval warehouses located all around the world. Supposedly there's a ton of stuff still stored in those warehouses; enough to keep us going without having to resort to trying to figure them out and building them ourselves.

And that fight that erupted at the Wilderness Camp? Well, that was as a result of something called 'withdrawal' from the dust. See, the drones now concentrate on distributing the dust over populated areas so what happens when you're away out in the woods is you get kind of sick from not getting the usual supply into your body. That also more or less explains why those stump-jumpers are kinda lacking in manners; they're not getting a regular full human dose every day.

But back to Micoazanon and what it really means. I'm writing this down from memory so I think I got it right but give me a break if I don't get it exactly correct. Micoazanon is a shortened word that combines, or I guess actually means, Mycorrhizal Anatrophic Non-Coding RNA. In simple terms, it's just what I said before; a fungus that allows things to grow more efficiently and promotes healing while also containing instructions on how to better tolerate conditions, which means that each generation of living thing can tolerate and flourish more than the previous generation. And since humans have far longer generation spans than most plants and other animals, we're a bit behind everything else in adapting to our environment which accounts for those same lip diseases and facial lesions as well as the need for continuing the spreading of the dust.

I realize that I'm probably the only person living on this planet that knows all these details about humankind's struggle to survive, and it all came about through some innocent questions about the material used for my ancestral bracelet. If Geena hadn't seized upon my bracelet as the key to figuring out who really murdered Amber, Jellie, and Dorman, which then led to 'the truth', both about the murders and about the world around us, would life have been simpler or easier for her or I? That's a question I can't answer, but I'd have to say life for each of us would have been different, not better or worse, just different.

I've been pondering what I should do with this knowledge; whether to pass it on somehow to perhaps my son, or to just let it pass on with me when my time's up. And yes, Micoazanon also explains why there are only sons born in my family; just a quirk of random selection to always ensure that there are some males left on this earth to carry on the race. And then there's that one person every generation or so that just doesn't respond to the dust as fully as everyone else does which at least partially explains Sukey going off the deep end with jealousy and killing Amber, Jellie, and Dorman, and also explains that story of the stump-jumper that got killed with the arrows, or the teen that drowned the cat that Mr. Jivey mentioned.

Now that I think about it, I'm pretty sure I've already decided to just let the secrets I've learned go since I've never written them down in these journals before. I think I'd rather that people continue with the society that they've built here and now and not be concerned that somehow they're repeating past mistakes and therefore the world is going to end, again. I'd rather people make their mistakes and learn from them, like we are all taught to do, instead of being afraid to do anything for fear that they are repeating a past mistake. If you're carrying that donkey of second-guessing yourself around all the time, pretty soon all you can think of is that donkey, so why carry it around with you in the first place?

I've kinda summarized it as 'better to look forward because if you pay attention, you'll rarely trip over anything, whereas, if you're always looking over your shoulder you will certainly trip and fall flat on your face'. And I've lived my life and taught Greywolf to look at life that way because, as I maintain, one can always change the future, but there isn't anything that can be done about the past except vow to never repeat it if you've made a mistake.

The only thing I can close this with is what my father once told me when I was around eight or nine years-old:

"Happiness in your life must be earned through who you are and what you do in life. The joy found in accomplishing your own work and from doing good deeds for and with others, is immeasurably more satisfying than just being given something you think you want."

I think I'd agree with that one-hundred percent.

***

Author's Notes

I hope that you have enjoyed reading this short novel. I had been thinking of a similar storyline some time ago when my local newspaper published a multi-part story about the seismic instability of the area north of Seattle, Washington, USA. I seized on that as a starting point for describing a peaceful society that evolved from the survivors of that seismic event and then, how they face the then unheard-of crime of murder. It took quite a while fleshing out the story as well as coming up with the characters but I, at least, think it is a pretty decent story.

And for those of you that aren't familiar with the area around Seattle, I took the names of a couple towns in the foothills of the Cascade Mountain Range and made portmanteau names for the towns, e.g., the existing town of Sultan, Washington became Sultanawash while Mrs. Lambskin was a Deputy Prosecutor of the Greater Washida territory, or in today's terms, of the greater Washington-Idaho territory. So, I used a bit of literary license and I hope no-one is offended.

I hope that I have entertained you for at least a short period while you read this story. If you have any comments to make, please review this specific book when you visit my Author's Page on Amazon.com (https://www.amazon.com/stores/W.L.W.-Borowiecki/author/B01IS3RIBE?ref=ap_rdr&store_ref=ap_rdr&isDramIntegrated=true&shoppingPortalEnabled=true) and let me know.

I can't write anything you will *want* to read without knowing what you have *enjoyed* reading.

Made in the USA
Middletown, DE
25 April 2023

29204141R00086